W9-AMS-554

PRESENTED TO THE
Nashville Public Library
**A Gift to the Children of Nashville
from Taylor Swift
and Scholastic Inc**

DISCARDED

GREGOR

AND THE
MARKS OF SECRET

Also by Suzanne Collins

GREGOR THE OVERLANDER
✣BOOK ONE IN THE UNDERLAND CHRONICLES✣

GREGOR AND THE PROPHECY OF BANE
✣BOOK TWO IN THE UNDERLAND CHRONICLES✣

GREGOR AND THE CURSE OF THE WARMBLOODS
✣BOOK THREE IN THE UNDERLAND CHRONICLES✣

GREGOR
AND THE
MARKS OF SECRET

SUZANNE COLLINS

SCHOLASTIC INC.
New York   Toronto   London   Auckland   Sydney
Mexico City   New Delhi   Hong Kong   Buenos Aires

No part of this publication may be reproduced, stored in a retrieval system, or transmitted in any form or by any means, electronic, mechanical, photocopying, recording, or otherwise, without written permission of the publisher. For information regarding permission, write to Scholastic Inc., Attention: Permissions Department, 557 Broadway, New York, NY 10012.

ISBN-13: 978-0-439-87726-8
ISBN-10: 0-439-87726-1

Copyright © 2006 by Suzanne Collins. All rights reserved. Published by Scholastic Inc. SCHOLASTIC and associated logos are trademarks and/or registered trademarks of Scholastic Inc.

12 11 10 9 8 7 6 5 4 3 2   6 7 8 9 10 11/0

Printed in the U.S.A.   23

First Scholastic paperback printing, October 2006

The text type was set in 12-pt. Sabon.

For Rosemary Stimola,
Kate Egan, and Liz Szabla

PART 1

The Crown

CHAPTER

1

Gregor sat on his bed tracing the scars with his fingertips. There were two different kinds. The thin lines crisscrossing his arms had been left by the treacherous vines that had tried to drag him into the Underland jungle. And the deeper marks — the ones made by the mandibles of gigantic ants during a battle — they could be found on most of the rest of his body, although his legs had borne the brunt of the attack. The scars had flattened out a little, but the silvery white color made them far too noticeable for him to wear short sleeves or cutoffs. While none of this had mattered when it was cold out and he had had to wear warm clothing, in the ninety-plus temperatures of July it was a real issue.

He made a face as he took a small stone jar off his

windowsill and unscrewed the lid. The fishy smell of the ointment immediately filled the room. It had been prescribed by the Underlander doctors to help diminish the scarring, but he hadn't been very responsible about using it. Hadn't even thought about it much really until that day in May when he'd walked out into the living room in shorts and his neighbor Mrs. Cormaci had gasped, "Gregor, you can't go outside with your legs showing like that! People will start asking questions!"

She was right. There were about a zillion things his family couldn't afford . . . but questions topped the list.

As he smeared the gunk from the jar on his legs, Gregor thought longingly of the local basketball court, the wide, grassy lawns in Central Park, and the public swimming pool. At least he could go to the Underland. Knowing that gave him some comfort.

How ironic that the Underland, which had always been a place to dread, had become a place to escape to this summer. Their steamy apartment was crowded with Gregor, his bedridden grandma, his sick dad, and his two younger sisters, eight-year-old Lizzie and three-year-old Boots. And yet there was always the sense that someone was missing . . . the empty chair at the kitchen table . . . the unused toothbrush in the holder . . . sometimes Gregor would catch himself wandering from room to room aimlessly looking for something and then realize he was just hoping to find his mom.

She was better off in the Underland in a lot of ways. Even if it was miles beneath their apartment and she missed them all so much. The human city of Regalia had doctors and plenty of good food — the temperature was always comfortable. The people down there treated his mom like a queen. If you could get around the fact that the city was always on the brink of war, it wasn't a half-bad vacation spot.

Gregor went into the bathroom to scrub his hands with the only thing that seemed to be able to cut through the fish ointment. Scouring powder. Then he headed on into the kitchen to get breakfast going.

A pleasant surprise awaited him. Mrs. Cormaci was there already, scrambling eggs and pouring juice. A big box of powdered doughnuts sat on the table. Boots sat in her booster seat with a ring of white sugar around her mouth, munching on a doughnut. Lizzie was pretending to nibble her eggs.

"Hey, what's the special occasion?" asked Gregor.

"Lizzie goes to camp!" said Boots.

"That's right, young lady," said Mrs. Cormaci. "And we're making sure she gets a big breakfast before she goes."

"A beeg breakfast," agreed Boots. She poked a sticky paw into the box of doughnuts and held one out to Lizzie.

"I've got one, Boots," said Lizzie. She hadn't even touched her doughnut. Gregor knew she was probably too nervous to eat, with camp and all.

"I don't," said Gregor. He caught Boots's wrist, directed the doughnut toward his mouth, and took a huge bite. Boots burst into giggles and insisted on feeding him the whole doughnut, coating his face with sugar.

Gregor's dad came in carrying an empty tray.

"How's Grandma doing?" Gregor asked, carefully watching his dad's hands for signs of the tremors that meant a bad day was ahead. Today they seemed steady, though.

"Oh, she's doing just fine. You know how she loves

a good doughnut," he said with a smile. He noticed the nearly untouched breakfast on Lizzie's plate. "You need to get some of that in your stomach, Lizzie. Big day today."

The words tumbled out of Lizzie as if a dam had broken. "I don't think I should go! I don't think I should go, Dad! What if something happens here and you need me or Mom gets sicker or what if I come back and everybody's gone?" Her breathing was short and rapid. Gregor could see she was working herself into a state.

"That's not going to happen, honey," said his dad, kneeling down and taking her hands. "Now listen, everybody here's going to be just fine, and you're going to be just fine at camp, too. And your mom's getting better every day."

"She wants you to go, Liz," said Gregor. "She told me to tell you about twenty times. Besides, it's not like you're going to go see her and —"

A look from his dad cut Gregor off. Stupid! What a stupid thing to say! Lizzie had tried again and again to work up the courage to go down to the Underland to see their mom, but she never made it farther than the grate in the laundry room before a full-blown panic attack hit her. She'd end up crouched over on the tile by the dryer, gasping for air, trembling and sweating. Everyone knew how badly she wanted to go. She just couldn't.

"I mean, sorry, I just meant . . . " Gregor stammered. But the damage was done. Lizzie looked devastated.

"That's because your sister's the only one in this family with any sense," said Mrs. Cormaci. She straightened Lizzie's braids although they were neat as a pin. "You wouldn't get me down in that Underland for a million dollars. Not me."

In a moment of desperation last spring, Gregor had decided to confide the bizarre family secret to Mrs. Cormaci. He'd told her the whole story, beginning with his dad's mysterious disappearance three and a half years ago. He'd talked about chasing Boots through a grate in the laundry room last summer and how the two had fallen miles beneath New York City to a strange, dark world known as the Underland. It was inhabited by giant talking animals — roaches, bats, rats, spiders, and a whole slew of others — and a race of pale-skinned, violet-eyed people who had built a beautiful stone city called Regalia. Some creatures were friends and some were enemies, and often he had trouble telling the difference. He'd been down three times: that first time to rescue his dad, the second to deal with a white rat named the Bane, and just a few months ago to help the warmbloods in the Underland find a cure for a horrible plague. Gregor's mom had gotten the plague, and no one knew when she would be well enough to come home. Finally, he'd told Mrs. Cormaci that there was a string of prophecies that called him a warrior — not just any warrior, but the one destined to save the Regalians from extinction — and that, after a few violent encounters, he had also been designated a rager, which was a term reserved for a handful of particularly deadly fighters.

Mrs. Cormaci didn't interrupt once, didn't make any comment. When he was done, she simply said, "Well, that takes the cake."

The amazing thing was, she seemed to believe him. Oh, she asked some questions. She insisted on double-checking the story with his dad. For a long time, though, she'd suspected that something very odd was going on with his family. The truth was almost a relief to her. It explained the disappearances, Gregor's scars, and the way Boots went around saying hi to cockroaches.

As to the fantastical nature of the Underland, Mrs. Cormaci could accept that. After all, this was a woman who had a sign posted by the mailboxes offering to read your future with tarot cards. Still, that first night, when Gregor had taken her down to the laundry room to meet a huge talking bat, even Mrs. Cormaci was a little bit thrown. She exchanged polite chitchat with the bat, commenting on the weather and such, and when some dryer fluff blew over and stuck in the creature's fur she didn't hesitate to brush it away, saying, "Hold still. You've got lint on your ear." Once the bat was gone, though, Mrs. Cormaci had to sit in the stairwell for a while and catch her breath.

"Are you okay, Mrs. Cormaci?" asked Gregor. The last thing he'd wanted to do was give her a heart attack or something by dragging her into all their mess.

"Oh, I'm fine. I'm fine," she said, patting his shoulder absentmindedly. "It's just the whole thing wasn't quite real until I saw that bat . . . and now it's a little more real than I was counting on."

From that moment on, Mrs. Cormaci had made it her business to care for Gregor's family. And they let her because they needed her help so much.

Now she finished arranging Lizzie's braids. "So,

your camp clothes are all packed. They'll feed you lunch first thing when you get there. How about I wrap up your doughnut for the road?" she asked.

"No, I'm sorry. I won't eat it," said Lizzie. "I want Gregor to give it to Ripred."

"Okay, Liz," said Gregor. He had an echolocation lesson with the big rat today. While Gregor didn't really like the practice of taking Ripred Lizzie's food, it was important to her and it always put the rat in a better mood.

Mrs. Cormaci shook her head. "There's a whole world of creatures down there having a hard time; they had the plague, they don't have enough to eat, somebody's attacking them. . . . How come you're giving your doughnut to some smart-alecky rat who's the only one who can take care of himself?"

"Because I think he's lonely," said Lizzie softly.

Gregor suppressed a sound of exasperation. Leave it to Lizzie to turn that irascible, lethal grouch Ripred into someone to feel sorry for.

"Well, you've got an awful big heart for such a little girl," said Mrs. Cormaci, giving her a squeeze. "Go brush your teeth so you don't miss the bus."

Lizzie left the room, happy to escape breakfast.

Mrs. Cormaci looked after her and shook her head. "Her, I worry about."

"Maybe camp will be good for her," said Gregor.

"Sure. Sure it will," said his dad. But no one really seemed convinced.

For better or worse, Lizzie was on the bus fifteen minutes later, off to the summer camp for city kids.

Gregor had about an hour before he had to leave for his lesson with Ripred. He sat down with his dad and Mrs. Cormaci to discuss what they called the family business.

Down in Regalia, the humans had a museum full of things that had fallen with their unfortunate owners from New York City. This had been going on for several centuries, so there was quite a collection. Because of his family's financial situation, Gregor was granted permission to take anything that might be of value. At first, he had combed through the old wallets and purses and scraped up every bit of money he could find. For a while, this kept them afloat.

But Mrs. Cormaci had bigger ideas. "I know this man, Mr. Otts. He buys and sells antiques." She gave Gregor a suitcase and instructed him to fill it up on his next trip. So, he did. Some of the items were worthless, but there was a ring with a big red stone that had paid the bills for two whole months. Now the money from the ring was about to run out, so they were in the process of planning their next sale. Everyone agreed it should be an elegant old violin Gregor had found under a saddle at the back of the museum. It was undamaged, still in its case. You could tell just by looking at it that it was worth a bundle.

Although Gregor was grateful for the income the items brought in, he did not enjoy his scavenging trips to the museum. Did not enjoy thinking about the wallets, the ring, the violin . . . the people they had belonged to, and what tragic ends they had met in the Underland. Only a few of the owners would have been rescued and taken to Regalia. The rest would have died from the fall or been hunted down and eaten by the rats in the tunnels. So, it made him sad, "the family business."

However, today's trip to the Underland did not require raiding the museum. He planned to see his mom, hang out with his friends, and stay for a nice big dinner. In fact, today should be fun . . . once he finished his echolocation lesson with Ripred.

"You better get going if you want to meet that rat on time," said Mrs. Cormaci.

"Come on, Boots. Want to go see Mama?" asked Gregor. He took a flashlight from one of the coat hooks by the front door and hung it on his belt loop.

"Ye-es!" said Boots. "I get my sandals!" She ran off excitedly. Unlike Lizzie, Boots was a big fan of the Underland.

Mrs. Cormaci offered to escort them down to the laundry room to act as their lookout. First she made them stop by her apartment for a minute. She opened the fridge and dug out a half-eaten bowl of macaroni salad. "Here," she said. "You may as well take it down to the rat."

Gregor held up Lizzie's doughnut, which he had wrapped up in a paper napkin. "I've got Ripred covered."

"What, it's going to break your arm to carry this, too?" asked Mrs. Cormaci.

"No. I just don't see any point in giving him a perfectly good bowl of macaroni salad. He can catch his own dinner," said Gregor.

"I was about to throw it out, anyway. I think the

mayonnaise is starting to turn bad. But I doubt he'll care," said Mrs. Cormaci. "Wait, let me find a paper bag. I don't want that rat licking my bowl."

Gregor shook his head. "You're worse than Lizzie." She could make her little speech to Lizzie about the doughnut, but Gregor knew better. Practically every time he went down to the Underland, Mrs. Cormaci made him drag along some dish for Ripred because it was "starting to turn bad."

"Well, maybe she's right. That rat, what's he got? No real home, no family, he has to fight all the time. You know, everybody needs a little joy in their life. For goodness' sake, take him the macaroni salad," said Mrs. Cormaci.

"Fine," said Gregor. He didn't know why he put up so much resistance to taking Ripred a snack. Yes, he did. Gregor wasn't good at echolocation, and Ripred's impatience with his lack of improvement had made him at first insecure and then defiant. He had basically stopped trying to master the fine art of navigating in the dark, and Ripred knew it. So the echolocation lessons had deteriorated into two-hour sessions of Ripred telling him what a weak, lazy loser he was. And the idea of rewarding Ripred with food drove Gregor crazy.

Down in the laundry room, Mrs. Cormaci made sure the coast was clear before she gave Gregor the thumbs-up. He opened the grate in the wall, gave a whistle, and almost instantly Nike's head appeared. Boots ran up and stroked the black-and-white stripes on the bat's face.

"Greetings, Princess," Nike purred.

"Greetings, Pincess," Boots said back, and then they both laughed. This had only happened about fifty times now, but it still cracked Boots up. Gregor thought Nike laughed mostly because his sister thought it was so funny. "We are both pincesses!" Boots exclaimed to Gregor.

"Yeah, that's . . . still a good one, Boots," he said with a grin. Being the daughter of the bat queen, Nike actually was a princess. The cockroaches called Boots "Princess" because they were nuts about her, but it was really just a nickname. "Come on, Pincesses, or I'll be late." He scooped up Boots and turned to Mrs. Cormaci. "So, we'll see you tonight?"

"Sure. You kids have a good time. I'll keep an eye on things," she said.

Suddenly Gregor felt bad that he'd made a fuss about the macaroni. How could he argue with Mrs. Cormaci about a silly sack of pasta when she was the only thing holding his family together right now? "Okay, thanks a lot, Mrs. Cormaci."

She waved at him dismissively. "What else have I got to do that's so important? Now you better get going."

The ride down the tube, through the dark stone tunnels, and to the brightly lit palace in Regalia was uneventful. But his disagreement with Mrs. Cormaci over feeding Ripred had put him behind schedule. The minute they landed in the High Hall, Gregor had to run to his lesson. There was not even time to pop his head in and see his mom as he sprinted down the steps past the hospital level.

Deep in the palace, Gregor removed four thick stone bars that secured a heavy door and slipped through it, leaving the door slightly ajar for his return. His feet carried him down multiple sets of stairs. The Regalian council had reluctantly agreed for his lessons to take place here where he was theoretically still inside the city limits, but where Ripred's presence could remain unknown to almost all of the people. The rats and humans had been warring on and off for centuries. Very few humans could deal with the idea of a rat prowling around so close to their home.

Ripred was waiting for Gregor in their usual meeting place, a large circular cave off a set of stairs. The rat was lounging against a wall, gnawing on some kind of bone. He squinted when Gregor's flashlight beam hit him and gave a snarl. "Get that out of my eyes! How many times do I have to tell you?"

Gregor redirected the beam but didn't bother answering. Even in the shadowy light, he could see Ripred's nose working.

"What's that smell?" he asked.

"Lizzie sent you this," Gregor said, and tossed the doughnut at the rat.

Ripred easily caught it in his mouth and rolled it around, savoring the sweetness. "Lizzie. Why is it I never get to spend time with the nice members of your family?" asked Ripred. "And the bag?"

"It's from Mrs. Cormaci," said Gregor.

"Ah, La Bella Cormaci," sighed Ripred. "And what does the enchantress of the kitchen send me today?"

"See for yourself," said Gregor. He was about to send the macaroni salad sailing after the doughnut when he heard a scuffling in the adjacent tunnel. The sound startled him. No one was ever down here except him and Ripred.

"I told you to stay put!" Ripred barked in the direction of the tunnel.

There was a slight pause, as if the creature was considering retreat. Then came a sullen reply: "I smelled food." On the word "food" the low-pitched voice broke into a squeak. Gregor thought of his cousin Rodney, who everybody had teased when he'd become a teenager and his voice kept cracking between his kid voice and what was to be his man's voice.

"Who's that?" asked Gregor.

"That's your little friend the Bane," said Ripred. "After he maimed his last two babysitters, the job fell to me."

"The Bane?" said Gregor in surprise. He had not seen the Bane in months. He remembered the soft bundle of white fur that had huddled in his arms in fear. Last December, Gregor had been sent on a mission to kill him, but when he'd discovered the Bane was only a baby, he simply couldn't do it. He'd delivered the pup to Ripred instead.

"Can I come in?" the voice said from the tunnel.

"Oh, why not?" said Ripred. "Come on in and you can personally thank the warrior for saving your life."

Gregor turned his flashlight beam to the mouth of the tunnel, expecting a slightly larger version of the rat baby. Instead, he found himself looking up at an eight-foot mountain of white fur.

CHAPTER

2

regor's mouth dropped open. "Geez!" In a matter of months, the Bane had gone from a pup Gregor could carry to the massive rat before him.

"And he's not even full-grown yet," said Ripred. "We're expecting another two to four feet by Christmas."

"Like snow," Gregor thought. "'We're expecting another two to four feet to pile up on that big white mountain.'"

"You've met, but allow me to reintroduce you." Ripred pointed to Gregor with his tail. "This is Gregor the Overlander, the warrior who refused to kill you when he had a chance." Then Ripred gestured to the Bane. "And this is the rat we call the Bane, although his mother gave him a much sweeter name . . . Pearlpelt."

Because his pelt, his coat, was white as a pearl. It did have a strange iridescent quality, like a pearl, too. When patches of it caught the light, Gregor saw glimpses of color, pink and blue and green. In the Underland, it was not uncommon for mice and even bats to have white coats. But there was only one white rat. That's how everyone had known Pearlpelt was the snowy rat mentioned in "The Prophecy of Bane."

"Hey," said Gregor to the mountain.

The white rat shifted uneasily but didn't answer.

"So, what do you like to be called?" Gregor asked.

"It doesn't matter what I *like* to be called. Everyone just calls me Bane or the Bane except Ripred. He makes fun of my name," said the Bane. "Calls me Pearlpet or Pearliegirlie."

Ripred just shrugged. "It's a hard name to say, Pearlpelt. Practically a tongue twister. Try to say it three times fast. Go on. Pearlpelt, Pullpet, Purput. See? It's impossible."

"Pearlpelt, Pearlpelt, Pearlpelt," said the Bane rapidly. He locked eyes with Ripred. "He can say it. He just wants to humiliate me."

Gregor knew the Bane was right about that. Ripred was a master of humiliation. He hadn't been too bad to Gregor until that trip in the jungle, but he'd been awful then and it had continued right through the echolocation lessons. If the Bane was with Ripred full-time, he was probably a constant target. Gregor felt a twinge of sympathy.

"Ignore him. That's what I do," said Gregor.

"It's different for you. You're a rager," said the Bane. "I wish I was a rager. Or at least full-grown. Things would be different then."

"And tell us, please, how things will change when you're full-grown," yawned Ripred.

"I'll be king, for one thing," shot back the Bane.

Gregor felt a stab of uneasiness at the words. The reason he had been ordered to kill the Bane was to keep the white rat from coming to power. A prophecy had warned of the Bane's potential for evil. And here he was already talking about becoming king. That wasn't good.

"Oh? And who's been telling you that?" said Ripred. "Twirltongue?"

The Bane shifted his glance to the ground. "Maybe."

"She's very persuasive, isn't she? But I wouldn't put too much stock in what Twirltongue says. She once convinced me I was well liked," said Ripred.

"And my other friends," said the Bane.

"Your friends," said Ripred with loathing. "Anyone can be your friend if they give you a few fish. And they whisper their little words in your ears . . . how you're so strong and so brave . . . how one day you'll be king . . . and you greedily gulp down the fish and the lies . . . you big white fool. . . . You have no idea who your real enemies are."

"You're my enemy, I know that!" spat out the Bane. "You're every gnawer's enemy. Making deals with wretched humans and fliers and nibblers, when you should be thinking of ways to kill them off! Twirltongue told me how you turned on Gorger because you thought you could lead us. As if any decent gnawer would ever follow you. To the rest of us, you're nothing but a joke! I should, I should —"

"You should what? Kill me? You know you're always welcome to try, Pearliegirlie," said Ripred.

And then, to Gregor's amazement, the Bane let out a roar and attacked Ripred. There were very few rats with the guts to do this. Ripred was just too deadly. The Bane might be a few feet taller and a few pounds heavier than Ripred, but how could he possibly think he could take the older rat on?

Gregor took a running leap for the stairs to avoid the flying claws and teeth. The Bane was fighting furiously, but he couldn't even touch Ripred, who was knocking him around the cave without any apparent effort. Still, watching them go at it, Gregor felt afraid of the Bane for the first time. It wasn't his size or what any prophecy had said about him; it was his willingness to battle Ripred. He was either very brave or very stupid or just very deluded about his own power. Any one of those qualities was frightening in an animal that people thought might one day be responsible for destroying the Underland.

"All right, all right, settle down," said Ripred. "I'm getting bored, and when I'm bored, I'm dangerous."

But the Bane bellowed and lunged for him again.

"I said knock it off," said Ripred, deflecting the Bane so his head smacked into the wall with a loud thud. It was enough to stun the white rat for a moment. "You can't ever stop until you hurt yourself."

Apparently crashing his head into a stone wall had hurt, because the Bane gave up. He sat hunched over, running his paws over his eyes. Then to Gregor's surprise, he began to cry. Not just sniffles, but deep, body-shaking sobs.

"Oh, wonderful. Here comes the flood," said Ripred.

Seeing the Bane cry was somehow awful. All traces of the giant attack rat were gone. He seemed like an oversized, bullied child. "Why don't you lay off him, Ripred?" said Gregor.

"Because he hates me!" wept the Bane. "He's always hated me. He made me come with him. He made me leave my friends. I've spent my whole life as his prisoner."

"Is that what they tell you? Those wonderful friends of yours?" said Ripred. "And did they also tell you I spared your life and raised you from a pup? Were you fed? Did you get the plague? Are you here now to complain about me?"

"You didn't raise me," said the Bane. "Razor did. He's the one who cared for me."

"Yes, he's the one who cared for you, and how did you repay him? Tell the warrior here, before he starts feeling too sorry for you. Go on; tell him!" shouted Ripred.

But the Bane did not continue. Instead, he trapped his long pink tail between his front paws and began to suck on the end of it.

"Oh, boo hoo hoo, the poor little abused Bane. But

Razor treated him as his own pup. Went hungry so he could eat, protected him, tried to teach him to survive. And where is Razor now? Dead. And why? Because Pearlpelt here killed him over a crawler carcass," said Ripred.

"I didn't mean to," whimpered the Bane. "I was hungry. I didn't think it would kill Razor."

"For you to knock him off a cliff? Well, that is the usual result," said Ripred.

"I didn't think he'd go over the cliff. I didn't hit him that hard," said Bane, his words garbled by his tail.

"And then you tried to eat his body to conceal the evidence." Ripred turned to Gregor in disgust. "That's how we found him. Soaked in Razor's blood, chewing on his liver."

Gregor felt his stomach tighten in response to the gruesome image. He looked at the Bane with a new sense of alarm.

"No, no, no, no," said the Bane. Along with sucking, he began to gnaw on his tail, drawing blood.

"Yes, yes, yes, yes. Just in the past week you blinded Clawsin in one eye and ripped off Ratriff's foreleg. Why? You can't even tell me why! So now I've got to drag you around with me because no one else can bear you. Stop sucking on your tail!" Ripred burst out in frustration. "King, indeed! Do you really think anyone will take orders from someone who sucks on his tail?"

"Maybe they already do," the Bane hissed back at him. "You don't know anything! Maybe they do!" And with that, the white rat bolted out of the cave and disappeared.

"You wait where I told you to wait!" Ripred hollered after him. But there was no reply but the faint scraping of the Bane's claws as he ran away. "If he can find it," the rat sighed. "He gets lost if he blinks."

Ripred slumped against the cave wall a few feet from Gregor and waited a bit before he spoke. "There, he's out of earshot. Well, you've seen him now, Overlander. What's your opinion?"

It took Gregor a while to answer. In a few minutes he had experienced shock at seeing the Bane, discomfort at his kingly ambitions, fear at his boldness, pity at his obvious emotional instability, and revulsion at his murder of his caretaker. "He's a mess," said Gregor finally.

"He's a dangerous mess, and we let him live," said

Ripred. "You because you couldn't kill a pup. Me because I thought killing him would forever shut the door on any hope of peace. When you said no one would follow me if I killed him, you were right."

Suddenly it occurred to Gregor that he did not really know Ripred's plan. The very first time they'd met, the rat had made it clear he'd wanted to overthrow the reigning rat king, Gorger. Gregor had helped Ripred do that. But what was he after now?

"Do you want to be king yourself, Ripred?" Gregor asked.

"Not really," the rat almost sighed. "But I want the warring to end for good. And do you think the Bane is the one to put a stop to it?"

"No," said Gregor.

"Well, he wants that crown and there's no reason to think he won't get it. So what do you think we should do?" asked Ripred.

"Do?" Gregor had no idea what to do about the Bane.

The rat's voice was filled with urgency as he leaned in toward Gregor. "I thought maybe you were right. That I could teach him to be something other than what he was fated to be. But I got him too late. His father had already left his mark."

"His father?" said Gregor.

"Snare. You met him. You watched him and the Bane's mother fight to the death," said Ripred.

"Oh, yeah. . . ." Gregor remembered the horrible rat-fight in the maze between Goldshard, the Bane's mother, and the gray rat, Snare. But it had never occurred to Gregor that Snare was the Bane's father. There was nothing paternal about him.

"Snare was a vile creature by anyone's account. Why Goldshard ever agreed to be his mate is a mystery. I warned her against it. She didn't listen. But she regretted it. Didn't you wonder where the rest of the Bane's litter was?" asked Ripred.

"No," said Gregor. But now that he thought about it, it was strange that the Bane had been the only pup.

"Snare killed them. Right in front of Goldshard and the Bane. He didn't want them competing for the Bane's milk," said Ripred. "It was totally unnecessary. Any number of families would have taken those pups."

"That's awful," said Gregor.

"The Bane remembers it, too. And that Snare beat

him. And that his parents killed each other," said Ripred. "You would have thought he'd been too little, but you need only mention Snare's name if you want to watch him tremble."

"Do you really think he could end up as king?" asked Gregor.

"He will find followers, because he's the Bane. He's got the white coat, and the size, and enough hatred brewing inside him to wipe out the Underland as we know it. Most rats will overlook the fact that he's unbalanced, because he'll be telling them exactly what they want to hear. They've been starved too long, and then so many died from the plague . . . especially the pups. No, the gnawers won't care who he is or what he does if he brings them revenge," said Ripred.

A chill had been rising up Gregor's spine as Ripred spoke. Gregor tried to connect the giant white rat — sullen, vicious, violent, pathetic — with the baby he had spared. Remembered the Bane nuzzling his dead mother, trying to get her to respond. "Maybe if Goldshard had lived," said Gregor, "maybe he would have been okay."

"But she didn't, so we'll never know," said Ripred.

He shook his head and sunk back against the cave wall. "Razor took good care of him, though. And whatever conclusions you may draw from today's little drama, I was not unkind to him as a pup." Ripred's eyes burned into the darkness. His claws agitatedly groomed the fur on his chest, smoothing it down around the edges of the big scar he'd received on the journey to save Gregor's father. Ripred's shoulders hunched as if some heavy burden rested upon them. He looked miserable.

Gregor thought about what Mrs. Cormaci said about everyone needing some joy in their life. He held out the bag of macaroni salad. "Here."

Ripred took the bag and stuck his snout into it. After a few bites, he balled up the paper sack and ate that, too. The food seemed to shift his mood. His muscles relaxed, and he made a sound of resignation. "Hrm. Well, I guess there's nothing else to be done. Waiting won't make it easier. We may as well get it over with."

"What?" asked Gregor. "What do we have to do?"

"Haven't you been listening to me?" said Ripred.

Gregor had, but he was still at a loss. "I know the Bane's a problem. . . ." he began.

Ripred laid a paw on Gregor's shoulder, cutting him off. Gregor could see his reflection in the rat's shiny black eyes. Tiny and distorted.

"We have to kill him, Warrior," whispered Ripred. "And the sooner the better."

"Kill him?" asked Gregor in shock. He was thinking more along the lines that the Bane needed some sort of counseling or to be placed under some kind of watch. Yes, he was a mess, maybe even a little crazy, but look what he'd been through. And Gregor didn't believe the Bane had intended to push Razor off that cliff. Not with all that crying and tail sucking. Of course, the cannibalism part was sickening, but for all Gregor knew, rats ate rats. On his first quest, they'd watched one spider eat another, and Ripred hadn't had a problem with that. As to the Bane's hurting the other rats . . . well, the rats fought all the time. Did the Bane just need someone to help him learn to restrain himself? To Gregor, who was a rager who had not yet "learned to control his powers," condemning the white rat to death seemed pretty harsh.

"Yes, kill him. And we can't afford to wait long," said Ripred.

"But . . . I already had a chance to kill him. I didn't do it, remember?" said Gregor.

"Things were different then," said Ripred.

Gregor's brain could not process what Ripred was saying this quickly. He tried to stall. "If you want him dead so bad, why don't you just kill him yourself?"

"Because of the prophecy," said Ripred.

Prophecy? As far as Gregor knew, there was no prophecy. In fact, one of the few things that had made his life easier of late was that there had been no prophecy hanging over his head. No warning from Bartholomew of Sandwich, the founder of Regalia, who had carved a roomful of dire prophecies in the palace hundreds of years ago. As the warrior, Gregor had been mentioned in three prophecies so far. It wasn't impossible that there were more. Then again . . .

"I haven't heard of any prophecy," said Gregor. Maybe this was just another of Ripred's half-truths, like the one he had used to lure Gregor into the Underland to search for the cure to the plague.

"We all thought you could use a break after the last two hit you back-to-back. But trust me, it's there," said Ripred. "It's called 'The Prophecy of Time.'"

"And it says I kill the Bane?" said Gregor.

"That's my interpretation, yes. But don't worry; I'll be there to help you," said Ripred. The rat began to pace as he worked out his plan. "Listen, we'll do it tomorrow during your lesson. Bring your sword," he said. "And don't tell anyone about this!"

Gregor didn't like the sound of that. "Not even Vikus?" The old man was the head of the Regalian council, grandfather to his friend Luxa, who was the reigning queen of Regalia. Most important, he was one of the few Underlanders who Gregor was sure was looking out for him.

"Especially not Vikus. He'd be beside himself if he knew I'd brought the Bane down here. The council doesn't even want *me* down here. Anything you tell Vikus now, he'll feel obligated to tell the council. He's become practically useless to us because he's so guilt ridden over his wife's involvement with the plague," said Ripred. "So tomorrow, same time, same place. You bring your sword and we'll dispose of him."

Gregor pressed his lips together. To argue with

Ripred now would be pointless. The rat had obviously worked through the whole necessity of killing the Bane already. It was better not to put up any resistance until he could figure out what to do. Because if there was one thing he did not feel right about, it was secretly teaming up with Ripred in some cave and basically murdering the Bane.

"I'll see you then," was all Gregor said.

"I'm glad you understand, Gregor. We simply have no choice." With that, Ripred melted into the shadows.

Gregor slowly made his way back up to the city, his head in a whirl.

"Overlander!" The voice brought Gregor back to attention. He had automatically gone to the hospital floor. He saw Howard standing outside his mom's room. Gregor could never look at his friend without comparing him to the preplague Howard, who had been healthy and stocky, with unblemished skin. Several months after he had barely evaded death, he was still twenty pounds under his normal weight. The purple scars that pitted his skin would never leave, although the doctors were optimistic that they would fade some.

The illness had set Howard on a new path in life.

The Regalians had put him to work in the hospital, which was still overflowing with plague patients, and he was training to become a doctor. Howard was young and strong and had bounced back faster than most of the victims. But many were still struggling, like Gregor's mom, and Howard was committed to helping them.

"Overlander, we have a surprise for you!" said Howard.

"I hope it's a good one," said Gregor, thinking that one really horrible surprise from Ripred was about all he could handle that day.

"Come and see for yourself," said Howard, waving him into the room.

Gregor found his mom sitting up in a chair. His face broke into a grin. "Now what do you think you're doing out of bed?"

"Me? I've been up since six. Cooked a big breakfast, went for a ride on a bat, and now I'm thinking about rearranging the furniture in this room. Getting kind of tired of the décor," she said.

Gregor laughed. Of course, she had done none of those things. This was the first time she had even been out of bed since she had fallen ill. "Maybe you ought to save the furniture for tomorrow."

"Yes, in fact, we should get you back to bed," said Howard. "We do not want to overdo on the first day." He reached to help her up.

"No, Howard, let me try it myself first," she said. With great determination, Gregor's mom got herself to her feet. The bed was only about five paces away, but she barely made it, collapsing on the covers at the last moment.

Howard and Gregor hurried to help position her in bed. "This is most excellent," said Howard encouragingly. "Every day a little more and you will have your strength back in no time. Now I must make my rounds with the medicine."

"That's a good boy, that Howard," said Gregor's mom when he had gone.

"He's the best," said Gregor.

"He'll make a fine doctor," said Gregor's mom. "Maybe you'll be a doctor someday."

Gregor nodded, but he had never even thought about being a doctor. He had no idea what he wanted to be, really. Since he'd fallen to the Underland, it seemed like he already had a job. Warrior. But it was not a job he liked or wanted, and it was certainly not a job his mom approved of for her twelve-year-old son. She knew that the Underlanders considered him the warrior in their prophecies, but she looked upset whenever anyone mentioned it.

"Where's Boots?" he said, to change the subject.

"Oh, she visited with me, then Luxa took her down to the field to get some exercise," said his mom. "Did Lizzie get off okay?"

Gregor gave his mom the update from home. Lizzie off to camp. Plans to sell the violin. The heat wave. She nodded, eager for every crumb of information. He tried to think of more details to stretch it out, but his mind was largely occupied by his encounter with Ripred and the Bane.

"Your head is somewhere else today," said Gregor's mom. Her fingers found a purple scar on her cheek. This was something she did when she started to worry. Rub that scar. "What's the matter, Gregor?"

"Not a thing," he said.

Her look said she didn't believe him, but fortunately, Howard came in at that moment with her medicine and a suggestion that she needed rest.

"I'll see you soon," said Gregor, grateful for an out. He headed off to find his friends. If Luxa had taken Boots to the field in the arena, there must be a game or a training session scheduled. He hoped they weren't using the blood balls for target practice. Even on good days, he disliked watching the wax balls burst open, spraying bloodred liquid as the sword blades hit them. At the moment it was a little more violence than he could handle.

When Gregor arrived, he found a much more benign sort of training in progress. The toddlers were learning to fly on bats. At first glance, it looked like little kids were raining from the ceiling. But none of the raindrops ever reached the ground. The bats would fly a toddler high up in the arena and then flip over, letting them fall into the air. The kid might drop five feet or twenty yards before they would be swept up by a second bat and flown back up into the air.

Mareth was directing the exercise. The soldier stood in the center of the field, leaning on a crutch. The doctors had fashioned a prosthetic device made of fishbone and leather for his missing leg, but he was still in the process of learning to use it. Regalia's queen, Luxa, was assisting him, if you could call it that, because at the moment they were both laughing helplessly at the scene above. Mareth was pointing up at Boots, who was trying out the somersault Luxa had been teaching her. When a bat dropped her, she would curl up in a ball and rotate a few times through the air. But inevitably she'd lose control of the move and go careening toward the ground, flapping her arms wildly like they were wings. "Me!" she called out, as if to remind the bats she needed a lift.

"Stay tucked up, Boots!" Luxa called through her laughter. "Hold your knees!"

"I hold my knees!" confirmed Boots. She launched into another somersault that quickly deteriorated into her baby-bird routine. "Me!"

"Almost, Boots! Try once more!" called Luxa encouragingly. Gregor stopped watching the kids and the bats for a moment and just focused on her. He had not gotten used to the sight of Luxa looking happy.

Being stranded in the jungle for three months with her injured bat, Aurora, and a colony of mice had changed Luxa. She was so glad to be home, and her people were almost ecstatic to see her. It was as if for the first time they had recognized how lucky they were to have this twelve-year-old girl on deck as a ruler.

Luxa would not have the full powers of a queen until she was sixteen, but at twelve she had great influence and could now cast votes at the council meetings where policy was decided. While she was stubborn and gave the council fits with her attitude, Luxa was smart, strong, and unquestionably brave. A mutual appreciation had blossomed between the young queen and her subjects.

This all contributed to Luxa's happiness, but Gregor knew the real source of her joy was Hazard, her six-year-old Halflander cousin, with his lime-green eyes and black curls, who had been discovered living in the jungle. When his father, Hamnet, had been killed by an army of ants, Hazard had been orphaned. Luxa had brought him back to Regalia, and true to her word, it was as if they were now brother and sister. He lived with her in the royal chambers, ate with her, followed her like a puppy. And Luxa had allowed herself to love him.

Gregor spotted Hazard flipping off a bat high over his head. Hazard was older than most of the kids, but riding on bats was still a new skill for him. While the boy was allowed to participate in flying exercises, Luxa had strictly forbidden anyone to train him in weapons.

His father's dying wish had been for Hazard to be anything but a warrior, and Luxa had promised to fulfill it. While the other kids his age studied combat training, Hazard was developing his already extraordinary talent with languages. Ordinarily, the Regalians made no effort to learn other creatures' tongues. But Hazard had been raised in the jungle, where he'd tried to speak to anything that would speak to him. He'd come to Regalia with a fluency in Lizard and an ability to get by in several other animal languages. Vikus, who was Hazard's grandfather as well as Luxa's, had arranged for a group of tutors. Showing far more patience with the quick, willing Hazard than he ever displayed with Gregor, Ripred was teaching him to squeak in Rat. Temp, the cockroach who had rescued Boots from several disasters, taught both Hazard and the "princess" the clicking dialect of the crawlers. And Purvox, a beautiful red spider, had been shipped in to tutor him in her strange vibrating means of communication. In his spare time, Hazard would try to talk with the bats, although some of their sounds were simply too high-pitched for human ears.

As he walked toward his friends, a voice behind Gregor purred, "Jump." He took one step and leaped as high as he could in the air, stretching his legs out to the sides. The next second he was riding on Ares's back. Gregor always felt a sense of security with Ares. They were bonds, a human-bat team who had taken an oath to defend each other to the death. And after facing a string of impossible difficulties together, they were real friends, too.

"How's it going, man?" Gregor asked.

"Well. It goes well," said Ares.

Gregor ran his hand over Ares's neck. A brand-new layer of glossy black fur was beginning to conceal the purple plague scars. Gregor's bat, who had been the first victim of the plague, had not only managed to survive it but had also made an extraordinary recovery. Within a few weeks of receiving the cure, he'd been begging the doctors to discharge him from the hospital. Afraid that he would fly back to his remote cave outside of Regalia before he had fully healed, the doctors released him into Luxa's custody. So now he lived with her and Hazard and Aurora, in the royal wing of the palace. Gregor thought Ares probably preferred being with his friends to living in that lonely cave anyway.

"How soon do we eat?" said Gregor as his stomach rumbled.

Mareth whistled, bringing the bats and their small charges down to the field.

"It must be now, for the training ends," said Ares.

Ten minutes later, they were seated around a big table loaded with food. Besides Gregor, Luxa, Hazard, Boots, Ares, and Aurora, there was a young bat that Hazard had taken a shine to. Thalia. She was a soft peach color with white streaks like a tabby cat, only about half-grown, and had a love of jokes that Gregor found unsettling. He had modified some Overland jokes for her. "Why did the bat cross the river? To get to the other side." Something like that could make her laugh for, no kidding, ten minutes.

Today he told the old standby: "Why is six afraid of seven? Because seven ate nine." Unfortunately, she'd had a mouthful of food when the punch line came and nearly choked to death as she cracked up.

"Do you think she'll grow out of that?" Gregor whispered to Luxa.

"I hope so. Hazard has his heart set on bonding with her," she whispered back.

Gregor ate a hearty meal of grilled fish, marinated mushrooms, and fresh bread. He contributed little to the conversation, though, because he kept wondering about Ripred and the Bane. After dinner, when the others went back to Luxa's apartment to play games, Gregor said he had to make a trip to the museum. He really just wanted some time to think. Despite Ripred's warning, Gregor's impulse was to track down Vikus and tell him everything. But it was true that Vikus might go to the council. And most of the council members were jerks. If only he could find out what was in the prophecy Ripred had mentioned . . .

Nerissa! Gregor spun on his heel, heading away from the museum and to the stone room that housed Sandwich's prophecies. Nerissa spent much of her time there. If anyone could tell Gregor what awaited him, it was that girl. She was part of the royal family, Luxa's cousin, and had even worn the crown for the few months when everyone thought Luxa had been killed by the rats. But unlike her resilient cousin, Nerissa was thin to the point of emaciation, psychologically fragile, and had the ability to see glimpses of the future . . . sometimes. She was no more able to control her visions than Gregor was to manage his powers to fight as a rager. She often had no idea if an incident she saw was about to occur in an hour or had happened a century before. Still, when she was right, she was dead right.

As he had hoped, Gregor found Nerissa sitting alone in the prophecy room. Her physical state had deteriorated back to her prequeen days. Long tangled hair fell to her waist, and she was huddled in layers of mismatched clothing. "Greetings, Overlander," she said with her ghostly smile.

"Hey, Nerissa," he said, and decided to get right to the point. "Look, I was wondering about the prophecies. About me. Are there any more of them?"

"Yes," said Nerissa. "One in particular."

"Am I supposed to kill the Bane again?" asked Gregor.

She looked at him quizzically. "It is unclear. Possibly he will die," said Nerissa. "Why are you asking this, Gregor?" He didn't answer because that would mean exposing Ripred. "Someone has been putting ideas in your head about the Bane again. But you may tell this 'someone' that the prophecy of which you speak lies in the future, not our present time."

"How do you know?" said Gregor.

"Because events reported in it have not yet come to pass. It is possible they never will. As I suspect this 'someone' well knows. Perhaps he believes he can control fate, but he cannot," said Nerissa.

"She knows it was Ripred," thought Gregor. "Will you show the prophecy to me?" he asked aloud.

"No. It can be of no use to you now. In truth, I imagine it would be quite damaging. For your own safety and that of those you love, I believe you should avoid knowledge of it at all costs. Of course, if you would like to ask Vikus about it, there is nothing I can do to stop you," said Nerissa.

After a warning like that, what could he say? Besides, Gregor had already ruled out asking Vikus, so he just shrugged, like it didn't matter. "No, if you think it would just throw me, never mind."

On the one hand, he was relieved by the idea that at least temporarily he didn't have to deal with the issue of killing the Bane. From what Nerissa had said, it might never come up. On the other hand, Gregor realized that Nerissa's opinion would do little to sway Ripred. The rat, like many others, expressed a low opinion of her prophetic abilities.

Although he had racked his brain, Gregor found himself without much of a solution when his lesson time rolled around the next day. As he unbarred the stone door, he tried to review his plan. He would meet Ripred and try to talk the rat out of killing the Bane.

Gregor had little confidence in his ability to do this, though, so as a backup he went ahead and hung a sword at his belt in case he had to try to protect the white rat's life. The idea of taking on Ripred was ludicrous, but maybe Gregor could distract him long enough for the Bane to escape.

Knowing that if they fought, Ripred would try to take out his light immediately, Gregor had duct-taped a flashlight to his forearm. Instead of a torch, which would require a hand to hold, he had chosen a large glass oil lamp similar to the ones they had carried in the jungle. He could set it on the floor, if need be.

He mentally braced himself as he neared the circular cave, trying to sort out his argument for keeping the Bane alive. But when Gregor reached the meeting place, it was empty. No Ripred. No Bane. No one at all. He waited ten, maybe fifteen minutes. It was not like Ripred to be late. If anything, he had a way of popping up before you expected him. Just when Gregor was about to head back to Regalia, he heard a faint scratching noise in the tunnel the Bane had come from the day before.

"Ripred?" he called softly. There was no answer. "Pearlpelt?" The faint scratching came again. "Is somebody there?" Gregor set down the oil lamp and adjusted the flashlight on his arm. As he crept down a long tunnel toward the sound, he had the feeling it was receding, leading him away from the lamp, the stairs, and the city above. "Hello?" He entered a small cave. Another sound, a muffled laugh, came from his left. An unpleasant tingle ran up the back of Gregor's neck. Suddenly he knew he had made a terrible mistake.

He spun around, preparing to sprint for the door. Three rats emerged from the shadows, blocking his way. Gregor didn't recognize a one of them.

CHAPTER

4

Gregor's sword was in his hand in an instant.

The rats fanned out, making any movement back toward the palace impossible. But they did not assume attack positions. Instead they lazily flopped on the ground as if they were all about to enjoy a fun day at the beach.

Two of the rats had the unexceptional mud-gray fur that was most common in their species. But the coat of the one directly in front of Gregor was a beautiful silvery hue. This rat spoke first.

"So, at long last, we meet the warrior. Ripred is so possessive, the rest of us can't get near you." Gregor could tell it was a female by the pitch of her voice. And what a voice! Silky and low, with an unmistakable friendliness. Charming, that was the word for it. "You can lower your sword, Gregor, as you can see none of us are in a fighting vein."

Gregor didn't move his sword. "Who are you?"

"This is Gushgore and Reekwell," said the silver rat. Both rats gave a polite nod at their name. "And I'm called Twirltongue."

Twirltongue. So this was the rat who had been telling the Bane he should be king. What had Ripred called her? Very persuasive?

"You're the Bane's friends," said Gregor.

"You've met the Bane?" asked Twirltongue.

"Yeah, I met him when —" Gregor stopped himself. Why was he telling this rat anything? He knew Ripred didn't trust her. The question had been so casual, Gregor had almost told her the Bane had been here. "When he was a pup."

Twirltongue laughed. "It's all right, Gregor. We already know he's been here. His scent is everywhere. Not to mention his blood."

For a moment Gregor thought Ripred had killed the Bane without him. "He's dead?"

"Probably wishing he was. I would be if I were on

51

a road trip with Ripred," said Twirltongue. The rats laughed. "No, we found some drops of his blood. Been gnawing his tail most likely. Why would you think he was dead?"

"Because . . . you mentioned blood," said Gregor. Something about this rat kept him off-balance.

"Of course. So, you haven't seen him?" said Twirltongue.

"Not recently," said Gregor.

"Well, if you do, please tell him his friends are looking for him. Frankly, we're concerned. The Bane's barely more than a pup and Ripred is, to put it politely, somewhat delusional," said Twirltongue. "Not to mention dreadful company, but I don't have to tell you that after your jungle trip, do I?"

"No, you don't," said Gregor.

The rats cracked up and Gregor allowed himself a smile. After all the abuse, it was a relief, really, for someone to acknowledge how awful Ripred could be.

"I once spent four days holed up in a cave with him hiding from an army of cutters. By day three I'd begun to consider slipping out. I thought, 'Yes, I'll be torn apart by mandibles. But would it really be worse than listening to Ripred make up poems about me?'" Twirltongue began to recite:

"TWIRLTONGUE THE GNAWER
BELIEVES SHE'S A CLAWER,
BUT TWIRLTONGUE IS MORE OF PUP FOR

"SHE CAN'T FIGHT A CUTTER
ALTHOUGH WITH SOME BUTTER
SHE'D HAPPILY EAT ONE FOR SUPPER."

Gregor couldn't help joining in the rats' laughter.

"Not very witty, but it served its purpose," said Twirltongue. "I felt demeaned by both the poem's content and its inferior quality."

Gregor could feel himself nodding. Twirltongue had just nailed the way Ripred operated. "Like you were too worthless to even make up a decent insult about."

"Yes! Yes!" cried Twirltongue. The rats happily began to swap stories of Ripred's abuse, one-upping one another.

Gregor's sword arm relaxed and he let the tip rest on the stone. Sometimes he had to wonder about Ripred.

How well did Gregor know him? Maybe Ripred really was delusional about leading the other rats, about the threat the Bane posed, and about Twirltongue and her friends. Maybe Ripred was nuts.

The idea gave Gregor a jolt. Because if Ripred was crazy, then why was Gregor doing what he said?

Just then, Twirltongue rolled on her back, giving a luxurious stretch. "Oh, Overlander, oh, Warrior. How I wish I'd met you before Ripred did," she said. "But since I didn't, I think *now* would be a good time."

Gregor was completely unprepared for the attack. He just had time to dive to the right of Reekwell's lunge before the rat's claws scraped the ground where he'd been standing.

"No claws, Reekwell. And no blood. We need him to disappear without a trace," Twirltongue said pleasantly. "Break his neck."

There was no time to ask why they wanted him dead. Probably because he was the warrior. Shoot, his being a human was a good enough reason for most rats.

Gregor made it to his feet as both Reekwell and Gushgore came at him, whipping their thick tails at his neck. He backed up against the cave wall, fending off the blows with his sword. He began to sidestep his way along the wall, heading for the opening that led back to the city. If his blade made contact with the rats' tails, they pulled them back reflexively before they could be cut off. Gregor could not take a full swing and sever a tail because he always had another to block.

When the rager sensation began, Gregor felt his spirits lifting. Now he would at least have a fighting chance. His vision altered, zooming in on points of attack; his arm became indistinguishable from his sword. He could feel the rats beginning to hesitate and was just about to go on the offensive when it happened.

Gushgore's tail smashed the glass of Gregor's flashlight and the world went black. He lost his bearings instantly. Up, down, right, left had no meaning. There was only darkness and the sound of ugly laughter, so different from the kind that had followed Twirltongue's poem.

The rager feelings evaporated. Gregor's knees went weak and his heart began to race. This was it! The moment Ripred had always warned him about. Being trapped in a cave with rats without a light. Ripred had not exaggerated. It was the reason he had been so relentless about the echolocation lessons. Gregor was as helpless as a baby without the use of his eyes.

Gregor swung the blade wildly in front of him now but met empty air. He heard the whistling the instant before the tail knocked him upside the head and sent him sprawling sideways. He landed on his hands and knees and began to crawl frantically through the blackness, his sword clanking along the stone. "Ripred! Ripred!" he called desperately. Where was the rat?

Another blow caught Gregor on the seat of his pants and launched him several feet into the air before he slammed onto his stomach.

"It's over," Gregor thought. "This is it."

But as he lifted his head, a glimmer of light caught his eye. The last hit had thrown him into the opening of the tunnel, where he could just see the glow from the glass lantern he'd left on the floor of the circular cave. He was on his feet in a flash, running toward the light as fast as his legs could carry him. The rats took a moment to regroup, and then he could hear them behind him. He had a head start, but would it be enough?

The brightening light gave him hope, even as the rats closed in. He flung his sword behind him, and one of the rats cried out. With his hands free, Gregor pounded across the last ten yards to the lantern. In one motion, he swept it up and spun around. Just as Twirltongue leaped into the cave he smashed the lantern on the floor before her. The spilt oil ignited and a narrow wall of fire spurted into the air, blackening the fur on her muzzle. He didn't wait to see what happened next. He just bolted up the stairs to the palace.

Gregor burst through the stone door, slamming it behind him. His hands were shaking so hard, he could barely get the bars in place. When the last one was secured, his knees gave way and he sat on the floor, leaning against the door for support.

No sound came from behind the door. The rats had not followed him. Slowly he calmed down. As his fear faded, it was replaced by an overwhelming sense of embarrassment. He remembered himself crawling around on the stone floor. Calling for Ripred. Ready to give up. The warrior. In all his glory.

Gregor couldn't believe that Twirltongue had gotten him to doubt Ripred so quickly! Sure, he argued with the big rat a lot. But Ripred had saved his life repeatedly and he had only known Twirltongue for a matter of minutes. Ripred had not been kidding about her powers of persuasion. And if she could manipulate Gregor so easily, what could she do with the Bane?

When Vikus touched Gregor's shoulder, he nearly jumped out of his skin. "Pardon, I did not mean to startle you, Gregor."

Gregor hopped to his feet. "No, no problem. What's up?"

"I have been looking for you. I had a message from Ripred. Your lesson today has been canceled," said Vikus.

"Canceled?" said Gregor. "Oh, yeah, I went down to meet him, but he wasn't there. Did he say why?"

"He said he had misplaced something and had to go find it. You will resume lessons on his return," said Vikus.

Misplaced something. The only thing Ripred had to misplace was the Bane. Had the white rat run away? He had certainly been upset when he left the cave. He must have run away and now Ripred was hunting him down. Twirltongue and her pals must have just missed them.

"You know, Vikus, if Ripred can get down under the city, other rats probably can, too. All they'd have to do is follow his scent," said Gregor. "Are you sure this door's solid?"

"It has withstood four hundred years of attacks," said Vikus.

Gregor gave it a couple of approving slaps. "Good."

"Why does it concern you all of a sudden?" said Vikus.

If Gregor was going to tell Vikus about the rats, now was the time. But Ripred had warned him not to mention the Bane, and doubting Ripred had brought him enough trouble for one day. It was better to keep it a secret.

"Just crossed my mind," said Gregor.

For the moment at least, he had avoided having to confront the issue of killing the Bane. And after all, the Bane might escape entirely. If Ripred did find the white rat out in the tunnels somewhere, wouldn't he just go ahead and kill him? Or maybe Ripred would have a change of heart and try to help the Bane. That seemed the most unlikely outcome of all.

Gregor could imagine any number of similar scenarios, but as he lay awake that night, he knew he didn't believe any of them. There was a prophecy that no one wanted to tell him about. And that prophecy was about Gregor and the Bane.

CHAPTER

5

During the next few weeks Gregor traveled down to the Underland almost every day, but there was no word from Ripred. Gregor didn't know how to interpret this. Had Ripred just killed the Bane and moved on with his life? Or had he run into some kind of trouble? The rat was the most resilient animal in the Underland, but as the silence continued, Gregor began to wonder if something had happened to him.

Gregor could tell that Vikus was concerned as well. "It is not like Ripred to leave me in the dark so long," he confided in Gregor, who constantly fought down the temptation to tell Vikus all he knew. But he couldn't. Not only because Ripred had advised silence but also because the old man was so burdened by his wife Solovet's upcoming trial, Gregor didn't want to add to Vikus's cares. At first it had looked as though she might simply be reprimanded and perhaps dismissed from her position. However, as the actual death tolls from the plague became known, there had been growing pressure from not only the rats but the humans, too, that she be put on trial. People were saying that Dr. Neveeve, who had carried out the research and had been executed for her role in the epidemic, had only been a scapegoat. That it was Solovet, as the head of the Regalian military and the person who had given orders to develop the plague as a possible weapon, who should accept the ultimate responsibility for the plague.

So Gregor kept his thoughts to himself and tried to focus on the good things about his summer vacation. Like how his mom was getting better every day, and how Lizzie's letters said she actually seemed to be enjoying camp, and how there were really a lot of fun things to do in the Underland if you weren't being attacked. Swimming, exploring caves, playing ball games on bats. Sometimes there were even parties.

One morning, just as he and Boots had landed in

the High Hall, Hazard came running up to Gregor excitedly with a small scroll in his hand. "It's an invitation! To my birthday party! For turning seven! You will come, won't you?" he burst out before Gregor even had a chance to open it.

"Sure, we'll come," said Gregor. "So what do you want for your birthday?"

"I don't know," said Hazard. He looked to Luxa for guidance.

"Maybe he would like something from the Overland. Something we do not have here," she suggested.

Hazard nodded vigorously. "Yes, something I've never seen!"

"Hmm, I'll have to think about that. . . ." said Gregor. But he already knew what he wanted to get Hazard.

The violin from the museum had brought a good price. Enough to live six months. At the moment, every penny did not have to be counted. So, on the morning of the party, Gregor and Boots took the subway to the big toy store downtown to shop for Hazard's gift. Gregor found what he wanted at once. It was a plastic disc with animals around the outside of the ring. You spun an arrow around and pointed it at an animal, pulled a lever, and it played the sound the animal made. Since Hazard was such a whiz at imitating creatures in the Underland, Gregor was pretty sure he'd get a kick out of the toy. Boots found a little set of jungle animals to go with it, and then, because she'd been really good about not pestering him about it, Gregor told her she could pick out something for herself.

This was a big treat and Boots took it very seriously. She tested almost every toy in the preschool section before she saw it — a princess dress-up set. It had three pieces. A plastic tiara studded with jewels, a gauzy pink skirt with an elastic waistband, and a scepter that lit up when you pressed a button. Boots was overcome by the costume's beauty. "I can get this, Gre-go? Because I am a pincess?" she asked hopefully.

"Okay, Pincess. Put it in the basket," he said.

But she couldn't let it go. She carried it all the way home, hugging it tightly to her chest and occasionally murmuring, "*P* is for pincess." The second they got to their apartment, Boots had to put on her princess outfit, which was, in fact, fabulous, and they headed off to the party in the Underland.

Mrs. Cormaci had one of those cameras where you took a picture and it popped out of the camera and developed on the spot. She made Gregor stop by the apartment to get it. "I want pictures. And take some for the birthday boy so he can remember his special day."

Luxa had gone all out with the preparations. The arena was festooned in swaths of bright-colored cloth. Long banquet tables were piled with food. A huge cake, decorated with bats, cockroaches, and other animals, sat in the place of honor. And there were about fifteen musicians playing cheery music.

Hazard dashed up to them the moment they arrived, and Gregor let him have his presents then and there. He was so fascinated by Gregor's gift that he sat right down on the moss to play with it, pulling the handle again and again to hear the horse neigh and the turkey gobble and the dog bark. After several minutes, Luxa gently reminded him he had guests to attend to.

The place was packed with excited kids, swirling bats, and even a dozen cockroaches. The bugs immediately surrounded Boots, speechless with admiration for her princess outfit. Boots climbed up on her friend Temp's broad black shell and gave a demonstration of how the scepter worked, flashing it on and off.

"What on earth is that child wearing?" Gregor turned and saw his mom, bundled up in blankets, sitting in a chair near the banquet table. She was shaking her head in amusement at Boots.

"She's a princess, Mom," Gregor said. "You can't expect her to show up at a party in hand-me-downs." He gave his mom a big hug. "How's it feel to be out of the hospital?"

"Just like heaven," said his mom.

Gregor pulled out Mrs. Cormaci's camera to get some pictures. No one understood what he was doing until he got Hazard and Thalia to stop running around for a minute and snapped a great shot of the two of them with their arms and wings wrapped around each other. As the image slowly came into focus, the Underlanders were amazed. They had never seen photographs of themselves. The whole thing seemed like magic to them. When he rounded up a bunch of little kids for a group shot they stood up very straight, arms stiff at their sides, serious looks on their faces. Gregor made them say "cheese" about ten times, until they were giggling and had forgotten how important it was to be in a picture.

Luxa made an announcement that the dancing was about to begin, and Gregor quickly took a seat next to his mom. He was not much of a dancer even in the

Overland, and the last thing he wanted to do was strut his stuff in front of a bunch of people . . . doing what? Minuets or something? Something with steps.

But all the Underlander kids and quite a few grown-ups streamed into the middle of the field to join in. The first dance was called "Bat, Bat" and required a partner. A small chorus of people sang with the musicians, but a lot of the kids knew the words, too. Boots, who must have learned the routine in the nursery, was right in the thick of things, dancing with Hazard and singing:

"BAT, BAT,

COME UNDER MY HAT,

I WILL GIVE YOU A SLICE OF BACON,

AND WHEN I BAKE, I WILL GIVE YOU A CAKE,

IF I AM NOT MISTAKEN."

One person flew around like a bat and their partner had to coax them to their side by pretending to offer them food. There were specific steps and hand gestures that went with the words, as Gregor had suspected.

"It's weird. I think I know the words to that song," he told his mom.

"It's in Boots's nursery rhyme book at home," she said. "I used to read it to you when you were little, too. It's from hundreds of years ago."

"Oh, right," said Gregor. He'd read the book to Boots, too, but hadn't made the connection. It was strange to think that he and Luxa might have been hearing the same nursery rhymes when they were Boots's age.

The musicians did a few more songs, one about spinners making a web, another about being in a boat, and then there was a short break.

Flushed and breathless, Luxa, Howard, Hazard, and Boots came over to join Gregor and his mom.

"Why aren't you dancing, Gregor?" asked Hazard.

"I don't know any dances, Hazard," said Gregor.

"Sure you do," said his mom. "You know the Hokey Pokey."

"The Hokey Pokey? What is that? Will you show us?" begged Hazard.

Gregor held up the camera. "Sorry, I'm taking the pict —" he began.

"Of course he will!" said his mom, grabbing the camera.

And then to Gregor's horror, he was being dragged

out to the middle of the field to teach about two hundred people the Hokey Pokey. Not only did he have to do the motions he also had to sing the words until the musicians had picked up the tune and the general idea of the lyrics. Fortunately, Boots was beside him, enthusiastically shaking it all about, because Gregor just felt like sinking into the moss and disappearing. It didn't help that he could see Luxa and Howard off to one side, laughing hysterically at his obvious discomfort. The Hokey Pokey was doing nothing for his warrior image.

The song was a big hit with the Underland kids, though, and they learned it so quickly that by the time they'd repeated the number, Gregor was able to slink back to his chair.

"Thanks a lot, Mom," he said.

"My pleasure," she said.

When the next number was announced, the kids began to shout, "Who will be the queen?"

"Luxa, of course!" said Hazard, and ran to get her. She protested as he pulled her into the middle of a large ring of children, but she didn't really seem to mind. Why should she? Luxa looked as natural dancing as a bird did flying. As the children clasped hands and circled in one direction, Luxa spun in the other.

> "Dancing in the firelight,
> See the queen who conquers night.
> Gold flows from her, hot and bright.
> Father, mother, sister, brother,
> Off they go. I do not know
> If we will see another."

Next about a dozen kids joined her in the middle of the ring and mimed being nibblers, which was what the Underlanders called mice.

> "Catch the nibblers in a trap.
> Watch the nibblers spin and snap.
> Quiet while they take a nap.
> Father, mother, sister, brother,
> Off they go. I do not know
> If we will see another."

For the final verse, as near as Gregor could figure, everyone went around pretending to serve cake and pour tea for one another.

"NOW THE GUESTS ARE AT OUR DOOR
GREET THEM AS WE HAVE BEFORE.
SOME WILL SLICE AND SOME WILL POUR.
FATHER, MOTHER, SISTER, BROTHER,
OFF THEY GO. I DO NOT KNOW
IF WE WILL SEE ANOTHER."

The words did not entirely make sense to Gregor, but all the dancers seemed to know just what they were doing. He guessed a lot of kids' songs in the Overland were kind of confusing, too. Especially those old ones. "Hey Diddle Diddle" . . . "Ring Around the Rosie" . . . "Sing a Song of Sixpence." What did any of those mean?

A little while later, Gregor was at the buffet table ready to load up his plate when Luxa came up and grabbed his hand. "Come, Gregor. Hazard says you must be my partner for this dance."

"Luxa, I can't dance, okay? I think I've made that clear," Gregor said.

"But this is a simple dance, and the words tell you exactly what to do. Come, or Hazard will think you do not like his party," she pleaded.

Gregor sighed and reluctantly put down his plate.

"All right, but just this one dance." He let Luxa lead him out onto the field. Another circle was forming, but this time everyone had a partner.

"Start by bowing to me, and then just follow the words," said Luxa. Suddenly the music began and Gregor found himself bowing like some character out of a cartoon.

> "JOIN THE DANCE AND COME BE MERRY.
> TAKE MY HAND AND DO NOT TARRY.
> ONE, TWO, THREE STEPS UP,
> ONE, TWO, THREE STEPS BACK.
> TURN AROUND
> OFF THE GROUND
> AND SET DOWN WHAT YOU CARRY."

He didn't do too badly. That last part about "off the ground and set down what you carry" was a bit tricky. He was supposed to lift Luxa up, spin her around, and set her back down. He did it, about four beats behind everyone else, and then suddenly Luxa was gone and he was weaving around the circle, catching one person's hand and then the next, until he found himself back face-to-face with Luxa, bowing again.

"JOIN THE DANCE AND CONQUER SADNESS.

TAKE MY HAND AND BANISH MADNESS.

ONE, TWO, THREE STEPS UP,

ONE, TWO, THREE STEPS BACK.

TURN AROUND

OFF THE GROUND

AND GIVE YOURSELF TO GLADNESS."

Off he went again, making his way around the circle. By the third verse, while he would never admit it, Gregor was actually beginning to enjoy himself.

"JOIN THE DANCE AND BE LIGHTHEARTED.

TAKE MY HAND LEST WE BE PARTED.

ONE, TWO, THREE STEPS UP,

ONE, TWO, THREE STEPS BACK.

TURN AROUND

OFF THE GROUND

AND FINISH WHAT YOU STARTED."

At this point, people stepped back from their partners for one final bow. As Gregor straightened up he found himself looking into Luxa's violet eyes. Her cheeks were pink from the dancing. She was laughing, but not at him.

"You did very well," she said.

"Yeah, right," said Gregor.

At that moment two unexpected things happened. Gregor realized that he thought Luxa was pretty. And a gold crown dropped out of the air and landed on the ground, squarely between them.

Gregor automatically raised his head to see where the crown had come from. A big orange-and-black-speckled bat was circling above them. Gregor recognized him as one of the bats who frequently delivered messages.

"For you, Your Highness," said the bat. "Sent by a nibbler I encountered at Queenshead. She said that you would know its meaning."

Luxa laughed. "It means I was again forgetful of where I laid my crown, Hermes. I thank you for your trouble."

The bat flew off. Luxa picked up the crown and began to head off the field. Her hand lifted in the air to signal Aurora.

Puzzled, Gregor ran a few steps to catch up with her. "Hey, isn't that the crown you gave the mice in case they —"

Luxa clenched his arm and spoke in a hushed voice. "Please, Gregor, tell no one what I said that day. And do not let Hazard or Nike know the crown has been returned. They, too, may remember its meaning and speak of it." She looked anxiously around the arena. Hazard was happily pointing out the animals on his cake to Howard. Nike had been around earlier, but she was nowhere in sight now.

"So? Why can't anyone know?" asked Gregor.

"I will explain after the party. I beg you, keep your silence until I have a chance to speak privately with you," said Luxa.

"Okay," said Gregor in confusion.

Luxa took a few steps and leaped into the air onto Aurora's back.

Gregor scanned the crowd to see if anyone had noticed the odd sequence of events. Even if they had, only Gregor, Aurora, Nike, Hazard, and Boots had been present when Luxa gave the crown to the mice. They had been in the jungle, preparing to return home. To thank the mice for their kindness in keeping both herself and Aurora alive, Luxa had given them her crown and said . . . what was it? He remembered. "If ever you have need of my help, present my crown to one of our scouts, and I will do whatever is within my power to come to your aid."

Well, the crown was here, so the mice must be in trouble. But why was Luxa so insistent on keeping that a secret? If the mice were really in danger, shouldn't she be alerting guards or something?

She was back in less than a minute, flipping down off Aurora's back and landing beside Hazard with a cheerful, "Is it not time to slice this cake?"

Gregor looked up to see Aurora and Ares landing side by side in the stands. They huddled together, their heads touching as they exchanged some sort of information. What was going on?

A few minutes later Boots ran up to Gregor chirping, "Gre-go! Mama says we can do sleepover!" So, apparently they were spending the night.

"That's great, Boots," he said, and swung her up on his hip. He went over to check the news with his mom.

"Luxa suggested it. I guess there's a special family dinner tonight for Hazard and he wants you two to come. You might as well spend the night. We sent a bat up to the laundry room with a note for your dad," said his mom.

"Sounds good," said Gregor, but he knew something was up. He tried to catch Luxa's eye, but she seemed determined to avoid him. For hours. All through the rest of the party, through the family dinner, he could not get her attention.

Ares was no help, either. "What's going on with Luxa and that crown?" Gregor asked him as they flew to dinner.

"I cannot say," the bat responded. Which could have meant either "I don't know" or "I can't talk about it here." Gregor suspected the latter.

It was not until Hazard and Boots had been tucked in bed in the royal chambers and were fast asleep that Luxa opened up. They gathered around the fireplace in her living room, just Gregor, Luxa, Ares, and Aurora. Even though the guards outside her apartment were a good distance away, Luxa made everyone speak in whispers.

"The nibblers are under some threat. It must be significant if they sent back my crown, for they are resourceful creatures and have handled many difficulties on their own," she began.

"So let's go tell Vikus and get some help," said Gregor.

"No!" the other three responded as one.

"He would have to tell the council, Overlander," said Ares. "On so little evidence, and with so much chaos in the wake of the plague, they would not sanction action."

"But they would put me under guard," said Luxa unhappily. "Knowing this answer would not satisfy me. Knowing of my affection for the nibblers and that I consider myself to be in their debt. I would be watched constantly to make sure I did not leave Regalia."

"Even though you're the queen?" asked Gregor.

"Especially because she is the queen. They do not wish to risk putting her in danger again," said Ares.

"That is why we must divine the nibblers' situation on our own," said Aurora. "Perhaps with more knowledge, we can make a case to help them."

"Whoa! Okay, hang on a minute. So, 'we,' meaning the four of us, are going to do what?" asked Gregor.

"Fly tonight to Queenshead," said Luxa.

"Is that where the mice live? In the jungle?" asked Gregor. The name sounded vaguely familiar, but he couldn't place it.

"No, it is merely a landmark in the territory west of here. But that is where Hermes said he encountered the nibbler who gave him my crown," said Luxa. "I am sure she will still be waiting at Queenshead, expecting me to meet her. Will you come, Gregor?"

On the one hand, Gregor knew this was a bad idea. Not informing Vikus and the council. Sneaking around behind his mom's back. Man, if she knew he was flying around the Underland after hours he'd be grounded the rest of the summer. Not in Regalia. In his apartment.

On the other hand, nobody seemed to feel it was safe to confide in Vikus these days. Maybe the mice were really bad off. The other three would go, and if Gregor didn't, he'd be letting down not only his friends but also his bond. What if they ran into danger and Ares needed him? If they left right away, just to talk to the nibbler who'd sent the crown, could they be back before his mom even woke up?

"How far is Queenshead?" he asked.

"A short flight. We could be there and back before we were missed," said Luxa quickly.

"I guess that could work. But how do you plan on getting out of the palace without being spotted?" asked Gregor.

Luxa and Ares exchanged a look. "Henry knew a way," said the bat. "Aurora and I will meet you at the drop."

"Yes. Just give us a few minutes to ready ourselves," said Luxa.

They dressed in dark clothing. Luxa had torches, but they made a quick trip to the museum so Gregor could duct-tape a flashlight to his forearm. It was not supposed to be a dangerous trip, but after his encounter with Twirltongue and her friends he was so scared of being without light that he took all the precautions he could. They stopped by one of the palace's many armories to get a couple of swords. Luxa chose a light weapon with a long, thin three-sided blade that came to a deadly point. She had told Gregor once that she preferred this sort of sword because it was good for the acrobatic form of fighting she excelled at. Gregor picked a version of the heavier sword Mareth had been encouraging him to use in training. Its blade was flat, about an inch wide, and razor sharp. Then they tiptoed through the halls, avoiding the occasional guard, to a part of the palace that Gregor had never seen.

The entrance to the secret passage was in a nursery that had fallen into disuse after the large, cheerful one Boots played in had been built. The old place was a little spooky, actually. Sandwich had spent time in it as well as in his prophecy room, carving a menagerie of animals into the walls. It should have been cozy. But in the flickering light from their torches the stone creatures appeared threatening, their eyes too bulging, their fangs too prominent. Gregor felt trapped, not comforted. Even if you filled it with children and toys, it would not be a happy place.

"I have never cared for this room," said Luxa with a frown. "Fortunately, they had built the new nursery by the time I was born. But this is where Henry spent his early years."

"Maybe that's why he was so messed up," thought Gregor, but he didn't dare say it aloud. Luxa could speak about Henry more easily now. The wounds from her cousin's betrayal were beginning to heal. But the subject was still painful and nothing she could joke about.

"Here is the entrance," said Luxa. She stopped in front of a large stone turtle that sat up against the back wall. It reminded Gregor of the big metal turtles Boots loved to climb on in Central Park. Except it had a furious expression on its face and the mouth was opened as if it was about to inflict a vicious bite.

"Yikes," said Gregor. "Bet the kids loved that."

"No, they avoided it. Except for Henry, who rode on its back and made up fearsome tales about it. And one day, while the others napped, he found the courage to do this." Luxa stuck her arm into the turtle's mouth, felt around, and twisted something. There was a click and one side of the turtle's shell popped open ever so slightly. "He closed the shell before anyone could know of his discovery, but that night he returned to the nursery and opened it." Luxa lifted up the turtle's shell to reveal a stairway. "He showed me this when I was eight. It was our special secret, Henry and I." Sadness flashed across Luxa's face and then was replaced by resolve. "Let us go."

Gregor had to turn sideways to inch himself along the narrow staircase. The air smelled old, as if it had been trapped back in Sandwich's day and hung there ever since. Gregor had been wearing his sword in a belt, but when it first clanked against the stones Luxa made him remove it and carry it in his hand. "We are inside one of the palace walls," she whispered. "We must not be discovered."

It seemed to take forever to make their way down to the bottom of the stairs, where another turtle awaited them. This one appeared to be laughing. But the leering grin was even more unsettling than the angry turtle in the nursery. Luxa unlatched its shell in the same manner. When she lifted the shell open, a gush of cool, damp air hit Gregor in his face. He looked down through the hole. Nothing was visible, but he could sense a large open space. Instinctively he took a few steps back.

"What's down there?" he asked.

"The Spout. It is a lake fed by a spring. It provides much of the cold water in Regalia," said Luxa. "We must drop."

Before he could react, Luxa stepped through the hole and vanished.

"Hey!" he said in surprise, and leaned over the opening. There was no corresponding splash. He could not see Luxa, but the light from her torch reflected off the water about twenty yards below.

"Drop, Overlander," he heard Ares purr.

Oh, great. Another chance to hurl himself into a dark void. "May as well get it over with," Gregor thought. He slid his sword back in his belt and got a firm grip on his torch. He balanced for a moment on the edge of the rim, then took a small hop and began to fall. Ares had him in seconds.

It took about an hour to fly to Queenshead, which turned out to be a large rock formation in the center of a cavern. The rock did vaguely resemble a woman's head with a crown on it, but only if you weren't being too particular.

As they coasted down to its base, he heard Luxa cry out excitedly, "Look, there is Cevian, Aurora! There she is!"

Gregor spotted a small furry form crouched at the base of the rock. It was a mouse who had apparently fallen asleep as it waited for them. "That's a dangerous place for a nap," he thought. "Anything could find you."

"Cevian!" called Luxa. "Awaken! We have come!"

Ares landed before Aurora, so it was Gregor who reached Cevian first. It was almost like he knew before he touched the cold, stiff frame and noticed the indentation on her head where a blow had fallen.

Gregor turned and caught Luxa by the shoulders as she ran up. He hated to tell her but didn't want her to make the discovery herself.

"She's not waking up, Luxa," said Gregor. "She's dead."

CHAPTER

7

"What?" Luxa shoved him aside and rushed to the mouse. "Cevian?" But as she touched the body she became still. "Oh, Cevian . . ." she said, and knelt down. Her hand came to rest on the creature's paw.

"It was Cevian who found us in the jungle," said Aurora. "We would have been lost but for her."

Gregor knew when Aurora said "lost" she didn't just mean lost in the jungle; she meant dead. Luxa and Aurora had been separated from their friends in a rats' maze during the quest to find the Bane. Completely outnumbered in a battle, they had held off the rats long enough to allow Temp to escape with Boots and then fled themselves. After several hours of being trapped in the maze's twists and turns, they had managed to find an exit. Unfortunately, it had led straight into a sinister jungle where Aurora had lost the use of her wing. The mice had taken them in and saved their lives.

"When my pain was very bad, she would sit beside me and tell me stories or play word games to distract me," said Aurora. "She was so determined I should not give up hope. . . ."

"I trusted her," said Luxa softly. The words hung in the air. Gregor thought this might be the highest praise Luxa could ever give someone. The list of those she trusted, especially since Henry's deception, was almost nonexistent. Aurora. Ares. Nerissa maybe. Gregor doubted even Vikus made the cut and was sure he didn't. Certainly Luxa hadn't trusted him a few months ago in the jungle when she'd been willing to let him sink to his death in quicksand because he'd showed up with a couple of rats.

Cevian must have been someone very special to be on Luxa's list.

"I'm sorry about your friend," said Gregor.

"I, too," said Ares.

Aurora gave a small flutter of her wings in reply, but Luxa had not seemed to hear them.

"Who killed you, Cevian?" asked Luxa, stroking

the mouse's soft ears. "For what reason? And why did you send me my crown? You are so full of secrets tonight."

Luxa rose and buried her head in Aurora's golden fur. The bat wrapped her wings around the girl. It was not a long embrace.

"This is not the time or place for mourning," said Luxa.

"We must go to the jungle," said Aurora.

Gregor was unprepared for this. "Right now?"

"Cevian is killed. We know not why. Only that she came to Queenshead because the nibblers are in great jeopardy. Since she cannot speak, we must go to the jungle to find those that can," said Aurora darkly. "We must discover what threatens the nibblers. We must avenge Cevian's death."

This was quite a strong speech for Aurora. She didn't talk much around Gregor, and then only in brief, quiet sentences. Despite three journeys with her, Gregor didn't know Aurora very well.

"Go back if you do not have the stomach for this. Aurora and I will manage the jungle on our own," said Luxa.

If he didn't have the stomach for this? Did she mean if he was afraid? Gregor bristled at the comment because, in fact, when he was upset the first thing that reacted was his stomach.

"You and Aurora in the jungle? That didn't work out so well last time," said Gregor.

Luxa glowered at him. "Go home, Overlander. We no longer want your help," she said. She swung onto Aurora's back. "After you return him, you know where we shall be, Ares."

Aurora lifted into the air and sped off, away from Regalia.

Man, Luxa could get under his skin! She knew he'd help her out in the jungle if she asked. Why did she have to turn the whole thing into an insult? A dare?

Ares shifted uncomfortably. "There are many dangers in the jungle."

"Uh-huh. I've been there," said Gregor.

"Even the plants will attack," said Ares.

"Got the scars to prove that," said Gregor.

"Luxa speaks with an edge because she is in pain," said Ares.

Gregor turned to his bat in exasperation. "Look,

Ares, we both know we're going! Let's just give it a few minutes so it looks like it was hard for you to talk me into it, okay?"

Ares gave one of his rare laughs. "Huh-huh-huh."

Gregor shook his head but then laughed, too. He stopped when his eyes fell on the mouse. "Should we do something with Cevian? I hate to leave her sitting out here. Something's just going to come along and eat her."

"We had best let Luxa and Aurora decide. She was their friend," said Ares.

"Yeah, I guess you're right," said Gregor. He noticed a crevice at the base of the big rock. "We could at least scoot her back in that crack. Hide her a little."

Together, they slid Cevian back into the hole. It actually did a lot to conceal her.

When Gregor turned away from the mouse, his torchlight fell on a mark on the ground. He had not seen it before, because Cevian had been lying right on top of it. Gregor squatted down and examined the mark more closely. It had been roughly scratched into the chalky rock. And recently, too, by the look of it. There was a straight line. At the top, going off to the right side, was a thin, slightly curved appendage. It reminded him of a flamingo's beak. "Look at this," he said to Ares.

"Do you think Cevian made this mark?" asked his bat.

"I don't know. Maybe. Maybe she was trying to write a word. Do the mice know how to write? Ripred said something about the rats not being able to hold a pen," said Gregor.

"Both gnawers and nibblers can scratch out a word if they wish," said Ares.

"Well, it kind of looks like Cevian started to make a *P,* but she couldn't finish it," said Gregor, tracing the mark with his forefinger. "*P* is for Pincess," he heard Boots say in his head.

"Perhaps she was trying to write a name. A *P* could also become an *R* or a *B,*" said Ares.

Gregor felt a pang of guilt. *R* is for Ripred. *B* is for Bane. They were both running around out here someplace. Could one of them have attacked Cevian?

"It is strange. I believe Cevian died instantly when her head was struck. She must have made this mark before she was attacked," said Ares.

"She could have seen her killer coming and started their name," said Gregor. "If she recognized them."

Both Ripred and the Bane were famous in the Underland.

"And then been attacked, yes," agreed Ares.

They both stared at the mark for a while longer in silence, but it gave them no more information.

"Has enough time passed for me to have convinced you to go to the jungle?" asked Ares.

"Seems about right," said Gregor. He swung onto Ares's back and they sped off.

In about thirty minutes, they'd caught up to Aurora and Luxa. When they did, Gregor and Luxa exchanged a glare and then ignored each other for the rest of the trip to the jungle.

The first thing Gregor noticed was the heat. The humid air hit him like a wall, and he knew that the ground below him had changed from barren stone to thick vegetation. Then he could smell the decaying plant life and hear the mechanical chatter of the insects. Gregor had nothing but bad memories of the place, with its poisonous frogs, flesh-eating plants, and stretches of quicksand. He hoped they could get in and out of it as soon as possible.

Their destination was a spring deep in the heart of the jungle. Gregor had arrived there some months before, severely dehydrated and caked in quicksand. A group of mice had lived in the area and, under their protection, Luxa and Aurora as well.

"Do not dismount yet," said Luxa when the bats touched down at the spring.

They sat quietly, surveying the area. The only good thing about the jungle was that it always had some light that was provided by the small volcanic eruptions on the floors of a network of streams. At least Gregor could not be thrown into total darkness here.

Nothing seemed amiss. "Nibblers! It is Queen Luxa! Will you show yourselves?" Luxa called out.

There was a ripple of reaction in the vines at the sound of her voice, but no mice appeared.

"We must check the caves," said Luxa, sliding off Aurora's back. She drew her sword. "I will lead. Then Aurora and Ares. The Overlander will cover your backs."

The Overlander, not Gregor. She was still mad at him for . . . whatever. Not showing immediate enthusiasm for the jungle trip or something. And who put her in charge? He was doing this as a favor.

Gregor tried to decide if it was worth an argument. One of them did have to lead and one of them did have to take the rear, and since she knew the area better, this lineup made sense. But it was only when he remembered that she had just lost a friend that he pulled out his sword and got behind Ares.

The path was familiar. Gregor knew it led between the spring and the cave where he had first seen Aurora lying crippled in pain from her dislocated wing. It was more overgrown than he remembered it, as if it had not been recently traveled.

When they reached the cave, Luxa called out again to the nibblers but received no response. With her sword, she cut away the heavy thatch of vines that concealed the mouth of the cave, and peered inside. "No one," she said in a puzzled voice. "It is deserted."

They wound their way down paths and checked several other caves. Luxa called out repeatedly, but there was no sign of the nibblers anywhere.

Luxa sat on a large flat rock at the center of a clearing, her eyes fixed on the mouth of an abandoned cave. "I remember we had not slept in several days when Cevian led us to this colony."

"Or eaten," said Aurora.

"Or eaten," agreed Luxa. She gazed up at the dome

of vines that enclosed them. "At best I expected to find the nibblers as we left them. At worst suffering the aftermath of a battle. But that they have vanished without explanation is most disturbing."

"Maybe they moved somewhere," said Gregor, sitting beside her.

"The gnawers already drove them out of their home in the tunnels of stone. They barely managed to survive here," said Luxa.

"Perhaps they decided to join the nibbler colony near the Fount," said Ares.

"No, my uncle who governs the Fount forbade any new arrivals. He said the land would support no more. Besides, it is nearly an impossible journey to make on foot," said Luxa.

"Is there anyone around here we could ask?" said Gregor.

Luxa gave a wry smile. "Hazard could. He can speak the tongues of several jungle creatures. I regret none of us share his skill."

There was nothing to do but fly home. As they rose to go, something caught Gregor's attention. It was a small movement, almost a shiver, in the vines above him. He shot his flashlight beam up into the canopy but could make out nothing but the tangled mess of greenish-gray vines.

Suddenly Ares stiffened beside him. "Something is here," said the bat. "To our right."

"To our left, also," said Aurora.

"What? I do not see anything," said Luxa, flashing her light around.

"Look here," said Gregor. He shone his light on a patch of vines above them that had begun to undulate. "It's the vines. They're moving."

"But I know these vines," said Luxa. "They are harmless."

On his previous trip to the jungle Gregor had been attacked by carnivorous yellow pods and later drugged and lassoed by sweet-smelling tendrils that wanted his blood. He assumed anything with roots was danger-ous. "We've got to get out of here. Now."

The four of them hurried toward the path that led out of the clearing, only to find that the vines had woven together to close it off.

"Use your sword!" said Luxa. Gregor's arm was already in motion and their two blades sliced into the greenery simultaneously.

Something sprang straight for Gregor's eyes. At first he thought it was a vine with a thick arrowhead-shaped leaf on the end. But then the mouth opened and he could see the deadly pointed fangs.

His blade severed the head from the body just as he cried out a warning to his friends.

"Snakes!"

CHAPTER
8

Gregor, Luxa, Ares, and Aurora retreated quickly to the flat rock. Their attack had brought the entire canopy to life. It was a writhing, hissing mass of snakes. They were a variety of sizes. Some as thin as pencils. Others as fat as baseball bats. So closely did they resemble the vines that Gregor could still not distinguish them from the plants unless he saw the heads.

And there were plenty of heads to see. The decapitation of the first reptile had triggered a full-scale attack. Snake heads were shooting out at them from all sides. Flicking tongues, flashing fangs. Suppressing his fear, Gregor gritted his teeth and counterattacked with his sword. He thought of the blood-ball training back in Regalia. It was the same principle. Incapacitating the missile before it struck you. What he couldn't hit with his sword he deflected with his torch.

Only the largest snakes could cover the distance to the rock, but it was all Gregor and Luxa could do to keep them at bay.

With relief, Gregor felt the rager sensation begin buzzing through his body. He welcomed the adrenaline rush, the heightening of his senses, the giving over to his instincts. Ripred had been right when he'd said that there would be times that Gregor would be glad of the gift of being a rager. Maybe he was getting a better handle on the phenomenon, because today he was able to fight without losing awareness of his actions and without fear at his transformation.

Now, for instance, he was quite cognizant of the fact that Ares was trembling behind him. The bats were utterly helpless. Trapped in the dome, they could not take to the air to flee or even to fight with their claws.

"Make yourselves small!" Luxa ordered them. Ares and Aurora pressed tightly together. "The twisters cannot reach you with Gregor and me here!"

He hacked off head after head, but the onslaught only increased. Smaller snakes had joined in as well.

"The jungle!" cried Aurora. "It is shrinking!" She was right. The snakes were closing in on them. The dome was still intact but several feet closer on each side. Soon every snake would be able to reach them, and there would be no way to fight them all off.

"To the cave!" Luxa shouted to the others. "There is only one entrance; we can defend that!"

Moving as one unit, the four of them inched their way to the mouth of the cave. Gregor caught a glimpse of Luxa's blade and torch, whirling in some crisscrossing pattern as she held off the snakes while Aurora and Ares fluttered inside. Gregor and Luxa stood angled out, shoulders touching, backs to the opening, as the assault continued. For every snake they killed, another two seemed ready to take its place. It was only a matter of time before one broke through, one set of fangs made contact, and their defenses fell.

"This is no good!" shouted Gregor over the hissing. "They'll just keep up until we're beat!"

If only Ripred were here! Much as the rat infuriated Gregor, there was no better companion in a fight. Ripred would know how to get out of this alive!

Ripred . . . Ripred . . . what would he do? Gregor tried to picture the big scarred rat beside him at this moment. But he couldn't. Ripred wouldn't be standing in the cave mouth swatting at snakes. He would be, he would be . . .

"I'm going to try something!" yelled Gregor. "Get the bats out if you can!"

And before Luxa could object, Gregor was slashing his way back to the rock. He had no more than an image in his head. The image of Ripred, fighting off the humans in the arena, shredding the plants that held the yellow pods, in battle with the ants. When he was far outnumbered, Ripred always relied on the same fighting technique. He spun. He spun in a circle so fast that no matter what adversary reached him, they would encounter his claws. Gregor had only one sword, but he had a torch and he was a much smaller target than Ripred. If he could just spin quickly enough . . . !

The second Gregor's feet hit the rock they began to turn him in place. He spun with his sword in front, his torch straight behind his back. Faster and faster until there was only a blur of shooting heads, spurting blood, and twisting bodies. He stopped thinking, abandoned himself, and let his rager senses completely take over. At some point, the number of snakes lessened, but he did not let up.

It was Luxa's sword, thrust out to block his own, that finally brought him back to reality. The clash of metal as their blades made contact had such force that he broke hers in two. The second he stopped spinning, he was reeling wildly around the clearing, overcome with dizziness. He crashed into the vines, which were entangled with headless snakes, and grabbed hold of anything he could as the world careened around him. It was one of the worst feelings he had ever experienced. He thought he vomited but could never clearly recollect the moment.

Then a pair of claws lifted him into the air and deposited him on Ares's back. "No," Gregor said. "Too dizzy."

"Hold fast to my fur!" ordered Ares. "We must be gone from here!"

Gregor clutched Ares's fur and just wished for the whole thing to be over.

Time passed. The world steadied. Ares landed somewhere and Luxa helped Gregor off the bat's back. Gregor sat on the ground and tried to get his bearings. Luxa held up cupped hands filled with water to his mouth, and he eagerly drank. His heart slowed down. He was all right.

They were no longer in the jungle. Gregor gratefully felt the stone floor of the tunnel beneath him. He dipped his whole face into the cold stream, less to drink than to clear his head. When he sat up, feeling refreshed, the other three were staring at him uneasily.

"Are you ill?" asked Ares.

"No, not now," said Gregor. "I just got a little dizzy spinning around."

"Your mind . . . it is calm?" asked Luxa tentatively.

"Think so," asked Gregor. "Actually, I feel pretty good." He did. Like when he'd run miles in track and then gotten a buzz. Only this was a much deeper sense of well-being. "Why?"

No one answered.

"What's wrong?" he said.

"When you fought, it was as if something had possessed you," said Aurora. "Your face changed. You made sounds that were not human."

"I was fighting off about a zillion snakes. It was just that rager thing," said Gregor.

"I have never seen it before," said Aurora. "Except when you hit the blood balls, but that was not the same."

When Gregor thought back, he realized that was

true. Aurora had never been around when he was actually in battle. "Well, that's how I always get. Tell her, Luxa."

"No, Gregor, it was different this time," said Luxa. "Not like when I saw you fight the cutters."

"How?" asked Gregor. It had not felt that different to him. He'd felt a little more in control for a while.

Luxa chose her next words carefully. "You seemed . . . to be enjoying it."

"What? Well, I wasn't!" Gregor said. "And that's a really rotten thing to say."

"I did not mean to —" Luxa began.

"Let's just go home," he said. They scrubbed the gore from their skin in silence and mounted the bats. Not until he was up on Ares's back, away from Luxa and Aurora, did Gregor dare to ask, "What did I do?"

"You fought magnificently. You will one day be every bit the warrior that Ripred is," said Ares.

"See, that's what I was thinking about. How would Ripred get us out of there? That's how I came up with the spin!" said Gregor excitedly, and then stopped. Why was he excited? The whole thing had been a terrible, bloody encounter. It must just be the relief of having survived it. Or was it something else? "Why did Luxa say that about me enjoying it?"

"Because, as the fight progressed, you began to smile," said Ares.

"I smiled?" said Gregor. His skin crawled at the thought. At home, he never got involved in fights unless he was forced to. He had never liked physical violence and had a low opinion of kids who did. It sickened him to hit another person. "I smiled?"

"Overlander, do not make too much of this. Everyone knows being a rager is not a choice," said Ares. "Only it took us by surprise to see you so. As we know you do not revel in death."

Gregor didn't say another word the rest of the trip to Regalia.

They had left the torches in the jungle. Gregor ripped the duct tape off his arm and returned the flashlight to his belt, flipping it off. He wanted darkness to hide in while he tried to understand this new thing that had happened to him. But he didn't understand it. His postbattle exhilaration drained away, leaving him feeling empty and quietly afraid of himself.

He had a desperate desire to see Ripred, to talk to the only other rager he knew about what he had just experienced. But he had no idea where to find the rat. Ripred had taken off after the Bane; they could be anywhere. . . .

It was only when Gregor and Luxa were climbing back into the old nursery that he realized he had another problem.

"Listen," whispered Luxa, grabbing his arm. Footsteps were coming down the hall. They had been gone all night and well into the day. Both Gregor's mother and the Regalian council would freak out if they knew about the secret trip.

"Lose your weapon," Luxa told Gregor. They both quickly unhooked their belts and set them down on the stairs. Luxa flipped the turtle's shell closed, shoved Gregor onto an old pallet, and dove onto one about ten feet away. "Sleep," she told Gregor, and immediately pretended to do so herself.

Gregor had just flattened out and shut his eyes when the footsteps stopped at the door.

"Did Mareth have them check the old nursery?" he heard Vikus's voice say.

"I do not think this wing was checked at all. It is so rarely used," Howard replied.

"I believe I see a light," said Vikus.

Gregor had switched on his flashlight so he and Luxa could climb into the nursery and never thought to turn it off. Too late now, though. He could hear Vikus and Howard entering the room.

Vikus gave a chuckle of relief. "Ah, here they are. Slept the whole night here by the looks of it. Luxa, awaken," he said softly.

Gregor felt Howard's hand give his shoulder a shake. "And you, Gregor. Before the council sends out the army to find you."

"What?" said Gregor in his best sleepy tone. He sat up and gave a fake yawn. "What's going on?"

Luxa rubbed her eyes and blinked up at her grandfather in confusion. "Oh. Have we been here all night? I was showing Gregor the nursery. He started telling some endless tale about his bravery in the Labyrinth. I must have dozed off."

It took Gregor a second to realize she was trying to capture their normal banter. Trying to act as if they had not experienced the awful night behind them. He could play along.

"Yeah? You should hear yourself go on about how rough it is to be a queen," said Gregor, stretching. "What time is it, anyway?"

"Nearly luncheon," said Vikus.

"Good. I am famished," said Luxa.

"Come then, and eat. And I shall instruct Mareth to call off the search for you. What would you have me tell the council, Luxa?" said Vikus.

"Something very dramatic. Tell them I sneaked out at night, evaded the guards, and ran off to the jungle," said Luxa.

Gregor shot her a look, but she knew what she was doing.

"Yes. Very witty. See that you take better care where you sleep tonight, Your Highness," said Vikus. Then he left the nursery.

Howard remained behind. He was examining them closely. A little too closely. "That was a lively story. About the jungle. And it would have explained one thing," said Howard.

"What's that, Howard?" said Gregor, suddenly feeling cautious.

"This," said Howard. He reached his hand up to Luxa's hair and removed a piece of vine. It was small, only a couple of inches long, with three tiny greenish-gray leaves. Gregor had not even noticed it. Unfortunately.

"Oh, that?" Luxa coolly took the vine from Howard's hand and curled it around her finger. "I must have picked it up when I visited the fields yesterday morning. The council has asked me to familiarize myself with the maintenance of the crops, so that when I am queen I may quickly distinguish a good year from a bad one."

"Really? I know of no crop we grow that resembles that vine, Cousin. . . ." said Howard. "What is it?"

"Well, I am not yet an expert, Howard. That is why I must visit the fields," said Luxa matter-of-factly.

Howard's eyes moved back and forth between them. "You two look tired. You should get some rest." He gave them a smile and left.

Before he went to lunch, Gregor washed up in the bathroom and put on fresh clothes. The dark fabric and dim light in the nursery had concealed the fact that his garments were splattered with dried snake blood. Then he went to see his mom. By the time he got there, Vikus had been to see her, so after a brief scolding about being irresponsible, Gregor was allowed to go eat.

When he reached the dining room, he found Vikus, Howard, Luxa, Hazard, and Boots gathered around the table. The servants began ladling stew and passing bread.

They were just starting to eat when Mareth appeared at the door, speaking in a rapid, breathless voice. "Vikus, pardon the intrusion, but there is an occurrence of which we can make no sense," said Mareth.

"What is it, Mareth?" Vikus asked.

"Our scouts were patrolling the river that runs from the Fount," he said. "They pulled this from the water. It was wedged between two rocks along the beach." Mareth gestured to someone in the hallway. Two Underlanders came in hauling a large, round basket between them. It was covered with a tight-fitting lid. Water still dripped from its woven exterior. They set the basket carefully on the floor, and Mareth eased the lid off.

Inside the basket were half a dozen squirming baby mice.

CHAPTER

9

The mice were about the size of full-grown house cats back home. Their pink bodies were covered in a downy layer of gray fuzz. The sudden light seemed to pain their eyes, and they buried their faces in one another's sides. They were squeaking in fear and distress.

"Ooh, baby mouses! *M* is for mouses!" cried Boots. She wiggled off her chair and hurried over to crouch beside the basket and pet their fur. "Hi! Hi, you!"

"They are hungry," said Hazard. He took a loaf of bread from the table and sat beside Boots.

The two kids broke off bits of bread and fed the mice, who gobbled down the food ravenously. Hazard made soft squeaking sounds that were indistinguishable from the babies' noises.

Boots giggled as a little muzzle rubbed against her palm. "You tickle," she said.

But no one else was laughing. The Underlanders' faces expressed deep concern.

"You say this basket was pulled from the river?" asked Vikus.

"Yes, to the north of us," said Mareth. "It is one of our own making."

Vikus fingered the woven lid. "We send gifts of grain to the nibblers near the Fount in such baskets."

"How could someone have done this?" said Mareth. "Putting these pups on the river in this frail vessel. It is a miracle they survived."

Gregor had to agree. He had been on that river in a small boat. The current was so powerful, it churned the water to a white froth and carried along large boulders like they were Ping-Pong balls.

"If someone wanted to kill them, this seems an elaborate way to do it," said Vikus. "Who would go to the trouble to place them in the basket and set it on the river?"

"It was their mother," said Hazard simply. He fetched a bowl of stew from the table and fed the mice bites. "She put them in here and told them to stay quiet."

"Oh, Hazard, can you understand what they are saying?" said Vikus.

"Some of it. They talk like babies," he said.

"Ask them why their mother did this," said Luxa.

Hazard squeaked back and forth with the mice. "I can't tell exactly. Something bad was happening and all the nibblers were very afraid."

"Tell them that they are safe here with us. That no harm will come to them," said Vikus. "Put them in the old nursery. Have Dulcet care for them. And Hazard, perhaps you could visit with them from time to time so that they may communicate with us." He shook his head. "I must alert the council of this."

Gregor, Luxa, Hazard, and Boots accompanied the guards and the mice to the old nursery. Dulcet, the really nice nanny who usually looked after Boots, arrived almost immediately. She instructed the guards to bring in plenty of torches, and when the room was brightly illuminated it at least seemed less creepy. The stone animals were not so intimidating, and now Gregor could see that each creature had a fun little song carved next to it, like "Bat, Bat" or the thing about the nibblers. Except the evil turtle. Sandwich hadn't given it a song.

Dulcet cleared out an alcove in the room and fashioned a large, comfortable nest out of blankets. Then she sat cross-legged in the middle of the nest and spent a few minutes with each mouse, talking to it in a soft voice, cuddling it, and giving it bites of what looked like carrots. Soon they were all vying for her attention, trying to sit on her lap, rubbing their noses under her hand so she would stroke their heads. You would have thought that she'd been a mouse nanny her whole life. Of course, Boots and Hazard had to get into the nest, too. Soon the two kids and six mice were all snuggled around Dulcet in a comfortable heap. She began to quietly sing the children's songs from the walls. It did not take long for the exhausted mouse babies to fall asleep.

Luxa pulled Gregor into the hallway where they would not be overheard. "We must go to the nibbler colony by the Fount," she said.

"No. No, thanks," said Gregor, and started off down the hall. He did not want to go on any more secret adventures with Luxa or even talk to her, really. Not after what she'd said about him enjoying the slaughter.

"We must find out what provoked a mother to place her pups on that river," Luxa said, following him.

"Maybe she was crazy. I can't think of any other reason," said Gregor over his shoulder.

"You can think of no reason you might place Boots in a basket and leave her to the fate of the waters?" Luxa insisted. "Gregor!" She grabbed his arm and swung him back around.

"No!" said Gregor, wrenching his arm back. "Will you just back off?"

"You did as much in the jungle," said Luxa.

"What?" said Gregor.

"In the jungle. You sent Boots away with Aurora, who was wounded, and Hazard, who was but six. When the cutters came," said Luxa.

"Yeah, because she would have been killed if I hadn't!" said Gregor. Luxa's meaning was beginning to dawn on him. Something very frightening had been happening when the babies had been placed in the basket. The mother had had no choice. . . .

Inside the nursery one of the mouse babies had begun to cry out in its sleep.

"So you think the snakes attacked the colony near the Fount, too?" Gregor asked.

"No, the twisters cannot live outside the jungle. It is too cold for them," said Luxa. "We do not know that they attacked Cevian's colony, either. Only that they attacked us. The nibblers may have left for reasons that had nothing to do with the twisters, who then took advantage of their absence to occupy the land."

"I guess so, Luxa," said Gregor. She was holding out hope that her friends were still alive, but it seemed like a long shot to him.

"Something is very wrong if both the nibblers in the jungle and the ones at the Fount are in trouble. Perhaps every nibbler in the Underland is in peril. I need your help, Gregor," said Luxa. She looked so unhappy. Less than a day ago they had been dancing. Now Cevian was dead. The rest of the jungle colony had probably been eaten by snakes. The basket of baby mice had arrived indicating more tragedy, this time for the nibblers by the Fount.

Gregor could feel himself weakening. "Maybe we should just let the council handle this."

"They will do nothing. Not without days of deliberation," said Luxa. "I do not know if Aurora and I can face this alone. Please."

Whatever remnants of resistance Gregor had melted away with that word. "All right," he said. "Let's check out the colony."

There was no way to leave until the next morning. For one thing, Aurora and Ares were exhausted from the jungle excursion and had to rest. For another, Gregor and Luxa couldn't sneak out through the nursery now that the baby mice were there, so they had to leave by a legitimate route. Luxa decided the best thing would be to tell everyone they were going on a picnic, which would allow them to take along food for the long trip to the nibblers' colony by the Fount.

Gregor got permission from his mom to stay over a second night. Since he hadn't slept in two days, he was ready to go to bed as soon as supper ended, but he made one last visit to the museum to prepare for the next day's travels. As a precaution, Gregor kept a fresh supply of batteries in the museum at all times. He put them, along with three flashlights, some duct tape, and a liter bottle of water, in a backpack. These things were now standard supplies on any long trip. After a moment's consideration, he added a pair of binoculars he'd found when he was digging around looking for things to sell. They were real binoculars, not the toy kind, and seemed like a cool thing to have on a trip. Since most of the Underland was in darkness, he wasn't sure when he'd get a chance to use them. What he really needed was a pair of those infrared night goggles, but Central Park drew a lot of bird-watchers, not commandos.

As arranged, he met up with Luxa, Aurora, and Ares in the High Hall early the next morning. Luxa's eyes were reddened and somewhat puffy. He wondered if she had slept at all or spent the night weeping for her friends.

A couple of servants finished securing a huge picnic hamper on Ares's back, and left.

"I told the cook you eat like a shiner," Luxa told Gregor, giving the hamper a nod. "Shiner" was the Underlander word for firefly. Gregor had met two fireflies, Photos Glow-Glow and Zap, and they were both absolute gluttons and unbelievably obnoxious.

"Thanks," said Gregor. "So do you go around thinking of ways to insult me, or do they just come to you naturally?"

"It was the only way I could justify asking for such large quantities of food," she said, and attempted a smile. "Do you want to spend half the trip hungry?"

"No, I want to spend it eating like a shiner," said Gregor. He had swung a leg over Ares's back when a voice behind him made him turn his head.

"Going on a picnic?" said Howard. He was seated on Nike, who was just coasting in for a landing. The two had been spending a lot of time together in training lately, although they were not officially bonds. Howard's sword was in his belt. A hamper sat behind him.

"That was our intent," said Luxa.

"Nike and I had the very same idea," said Howard. "Shall we all go together?"

"Do you not have duties at the hospital, Cousin?" asked Luxa.

"I am free until the night shift," said Howard. "Surely you are planning to return by then."

What could they say? What could they possibly say to prevent him from coming along?

"Of course. But I am unable to invite you to join us, Howard," said Luxa. "Because . . . because . . ." She looked at Gregor for help.

Only one thing came to his mind. "Because this is kind of like a date," said Gregor.

"A date?" said Howard. The word was clearly unfamiliar to him.

"You know, when you hang out with just one girl. Not your friends," said Gregor. It was such an outrageous statement, he couldn't believe he had uttered it.

With really just the right touch of embarrassment, too. The expression on Luxa's face was indescribable. He decided to go with it. "Okay, see, now Luxa's mad because I wasn't supposed to tell anyone."

Luxa flushed bright pink, but she had no choice but to go along with him. "Yes. Yes. I thought it was a private matter."

"Well, it is. But do you want Howard coming along on our date?" said Gregor. Like he knew anything about dates! Not only had Gregor never been on a date but his mother would probably never even let him ask a girl out until he had finished high school. Once he had gone to a party at his friend Angelina's home and he'd been too shy to ask anyone to dance. But here he was. The date guy.

For just a moment, Howard actually seemed like he might be buying it. Then his eyes rested on the hamper. "That seems like an awfully large hamper for one . . . date."

It was ridiculously large. For two people. On a date.

"It is none of your business, Howard," said Luxa in a dangerous tone. "Go and let us be."

"I cannot. Though it be at the risk of intruding,"

said Howard. "You see, Nike and I, we know about the crown."

There was a pause.

"Hermes mentioned he delivered the crown to you in passing," said Nike. "And I told Howard its meaning. Of how you gave the crown to the nibblers in the jungle and instructed them to send it to you if they ever had need of your help."

"Oh!" Luxa literally stamped her foot on the ground. "You cannot come!"

"Let them come, Luxa," said Gregor. "We might need their help."

"Stay out of this!" said Luxa.

"I tried to, remember?" said Gregor.

"Here are your choices. You take Nike and me along on whatever mad scheme you have cooked up, or I go directly to Vikus," said Howard.

And as if on cue, Vikus appeared, an armful of scrolls rattling under his arm. "Did I hear my name? What is all this, then? A pleasure outing?"

"A picnic," said Gregor, Luxa, and Howard in unison.

"A picnic?" asked Vikus. "I wish I had time to join

you. That's quite a basket. How many are you expecting?"

A flutter of peach-colored wings drew everyone's attention, and Thalia landed in the High Hall. That could only mean one thing. And there they were — Boots, decked out in her princess attire, and Hazard running in to meet the bat. Temp pattered along behind them.

"Hazard, I thought you and Boots were with the nibbler pups," said Luxa.

"We were. But it is time for flying at the arena," said Hazard. His face lit up as he spotted the basket. "Oh, are we going on a picnic? You didn't tell me."

"It was meant to be a surprise," said Luxa. "I was just about to send for you."

"Well, mount up, then," said Vikus. He lifted Boots up onto Ares behind Gregor.

"Now what?" thought Gregor. It was bad enough that they were sneaking off to the nibbler colony on their own, but if his mom found out he'd taken Boots along . . . well, he'd rather face another round of snakes than that.

Temp skittered up next to Boots as Vikus settled Hazard on Thalia's back. "Enjoy yourselves and be home for supper," he said.

"Yes. Supper. Off we go!" said Luxa, taking her seat on Aurora.

"Pic-a-nic! Pic-a-nic!" sang Boots, drumming on the back of Gregor's head with her scepter. The whole princess costume thing had been a mistake. Next time he'd get her a coloring book.

They soared out over the city and then made a U-turn and headed to the north. Beneath them lay fields of grain, illuminated by an elaborate system of gas lighting. Underlander farmers were harvesting the grain with long curved blades attached to poles. The blades were like something people used in movies about olden times.

Once they had cleared the fields, a terrible fight broke out among them. Luxa laid into Howard for interfering, at Nike for telling Howard about the crown, at Gregor for taking Howard's side. She was probably furious about the date thing, too, although she didn't mention it. And she was absolutely determined to go on, even with Boots and Hazard along.

Gregor had plenty of misgivings about that part, but Luxa brushed off his concerns. "If there is danger, we will send them directly on to the Fount."

"The Fount? Where are we going?" asked Howard.

Gregor filled Howard and Nike in on all that had happened regarding the nibblers and on their plan to journey to the colony by the Fount.

"It is most troubling. But Luxa is right. Appealing to the council for help would be worthless. We must go ourselves," said Howard.

The trip to the nibblers' colony took at least twelve hours. For most of it, they flew up the wild river that flowed from the Fount down past the colony, past Regalia, and then emptied into the vast Underland sea known as the Waterway. About halfway, Thalia, who was still several months from being full-grown, ran out of steam, and they had to rearrange everyone so she could ride on Ares's back. Luxa took Hazard, Boots, and Temp on Aurora, and Gregor joined Howard on Nike.

It was during this leg of the journey that Howard brought up the whole date subterfuge. "Gregor, as Luxa has no older brother, I feel I must speak for her. As I would speak for one of my little sisters. I know you used what you called a date with her as a cover, but in the future you must think of an alternative."

"Why?" said Gregor, although he could guess.

"Because she is a queen, because you are an Overlander, because you are both too young, and because even if you were not, such a pairing could have no happy future," said Howard. "The process of finding a spouse in the Underland is a long and delicate one."

A spouse? This was getting entirely out of hand. "Howard, it wasn't a date in the first place," said Gregor.

"I understand. But for you to even mention it as a possibility shows how little you know of the Underland," said Howard. "Remember, too, that you expected me to believe your lie. And ask yourself why you thought it was a plausible one."

That pulled Gregor up short. He could feel himself blushing as deeply as Luxa had. At the time, he guessed he had expected Howard to at least entertain the possibility that he and Luxa might like each other. And worse still, there had been that moment when Howard looked like he was buying it.

"Dates aren't a big deal in the Overland," Gregor said lamely. They would be for him, but he knew kids his age who sort of dated. Went to movies. For pizza. Which was kind of like a picnic. Except inside.

"Well, they would be monumental here," said Howard. "Especially with my cousin."

"Got it," said Gregor, who was really ready to drop the whole subject.

As they neared their destination, Howard and Gregor flew ahead to scout out the area. The nibblers' colony began with a large open area just off the river. A honeycomb of small caves and a network of narrow tunnels flanked it. With its access to the river for fishing and clean water and its natural nesting places, it seemed an ideal location for the mice.

But there were no mice around today. Luxa's greetings were met with silence. The bats could pick up no signs of life through echolocation, either. For closer inspection, they had to land on the beach.

"This area officially belongs to the Fount, but my father allowed the nibblers to use it. He has always been sympathetic to their plight," said Howard.

"What exactly is their plight?" asked Gregor.

"They have great difficulty finding a home," said Howard. "They have been driven out of lands by cutters, by spinners, and most often by gnawers, who particularly hate them as they have always been our allies. They have ended up scattered in colonies around the Underland, trying to carve out a life."

"Well, then it seems weird they'd leave here," said Gregor.

"That is just the point," said Howard. "I do not believe they would leave here on their own. They must have been driven out again."

"We must check the caves," said Luxa.

What they found inside was spooky. Half-eaten meals. Rumpled nests. A pattern of small stones on the floor suggested a game had been in progress. It was as if one second before they'd entered the colony it had been alive and bustling with nibblers, and then *poof!* They had all vanished without a trace. As to where they had gone or what had compelled them to go, there was no clue.

By the last cave, Luxa seemed about ready to lose it. "What can have happened to them? There is no rhyme or reason to any of this!"

Just then Hazard gave a sharp cry from the back of the cave. They all ran to him, certain he must be injured, but he was backing away from something on the wall. When Luxa reached him, he wrapped his arms around her and held on tight.

"Hazard, what is it?" she said, running her hands over him to search for injuries. "Are you hurt? Why do you tremble?"

The boy pointed to the cave wall. Howard held his torch to the wall, and in the flickering light Gregor could see a mark had been hastily scratched into it. A familiar mark. A straight line with a thin beaklike appendage.

"Ares and I found this same thing under Cevian's body. We thought she was trying to make a letter, a *P* or a *B*. To spell out someone's name," said Gregor.

"No, no!" said Hazard in a shrill voice. "It is one of the marks of secret."

"What's that?" asked Gregor.

"A secret means of communication. An old collection of symbols that you could use to pass information to your allies but that were unknown to your enemies," said Howard.

"But, Hazard, no one has used the marks of secret for centuries. They have lost all meaning," said Luxa.

"Not in the jungle," said Hazard. "We use them. Frill taught them to my father and he to me. That is the scythe."

"And that means something bad?" said Gregor, nodding to the mark.

"It means death," said Hazard, and he was starting to cry.

"It means someone will die?" said Luxa, holding him close.

"Not just someone," said Hazard. "It means us! It means we who see it will die!"

PART 2
The Marks

10

Despite many reassurances from Luxa, it took Hazard quite a while to calm down. Even when they had left the cave and assembled on the shore of the river, he was still traumatized by what he had seen. Gregor couldn't think of any symbol that would be so scary in the Overland, but then compared to Hazard, he'd led a very safe life.

"What is a scythe, anyway?" Gregor asked.

"It is a tool used for harvesting grain. The farmers were using scythes today as we flew over the fields," said Howard.

Gregor remembered the tools then, being swung from side to side. "So, why do those mean death?"

"Because they cut down life. In old scrolls from the Overland, sometimes the figure of Death, in a hooded black robe, also carries a scythe. To cut down humans' lives," said Howard.

"Oh, yeah. That's where I've seen it," said Gregor.

Howard built a small fire to try to cheer things up. Unfortunately, in the ghost town that was the mouse colony the shadows the flames threw against the stone walls only made the place feel more eerie.

Boots, who was puzzled by the whole situation, squatted next to Hazard and patted him on the leg. "Hazard is crying. Hazard is sad," she said.

"It's okay, Boots; everybody is fine," said Gregor, picking her up for a hug.

"No, we are not fine. We have seen the scythe," said Hazard.

"And yet we still live," said Luxa, stroking his curls.

"Yes, perhaps that mark was meant for someone else," said Howard.

"Or they made it during the plague," said Luxa. "Before the cure was found and all warmbloods were as good as dead."

Hazard quieted a minute to consider this. "I don't know," he said. "In the jungle everyone dreads the mark."

"Did you ever see it yourself? In the jungle, I mean," said Gregor.

"Once. There was a swarm of flying insects. Their bite brought quick death," said Hazard.

"But you did not die, Hazard," said Howard encouragingly. "Or you would not be here to tell us of it."

"My mother died," said Hazard wanly. "Frill outran them, but my mother was bitten first."

There was nothing to say after that. No explaining to Hazard that they were safe. Around any corner could be another swarm of stingers. Another plague. Another way to die.

Some mouse had scratched that mark in the cave wall. Cevian had made the same mark at Queenshead. Why? What threat was upon them? Gregor didn't believe it had to do with the plague. Or the snakes.

"Hazard, when you lived in the jungle, how did the nibblers get along with the snakes?" asked Gregor. "The ones that look like vines."

"You mean the twisters?" said Hazard. "They avoided each other. The twisters eat the nibbler pups, and the nibblers eat the twister eggs," he said.

"It is true," said Luxa. "The twisters never came

near the nibblers when I was there. I believe neither thought it was worth the risk."

"So you think the twisters only moved in after the mice had left?" asked Howard.

"That is my hope," said Luxa. "But also my fear. It would mean that not one but two colonies of nibblers have left their homes because of an unknown threat."

"It sounds as if they have a lot of enemies," said Gregor. "The spinners, the cutters —"

"Those were land disputes. Once the nibblers had left their regions, neither the spinners nor cutters had any interest in pursuing them. I can think of only one animal that would do that," said Howard.

No one had to mention the rats. They all knew who Howard was talking about.

They had snacked from the picnic baskets on the flight, mostly eating whatever was on top. Now Howard laid out the delicacies the cook had prepared. Spicy fish salads, a dozen kinds of cheese, pickled vegetables, roasted chicken, sliced beef, stuffed eggs, several loaves of bread, and a variety of sweets. It was an amazing spread, but no one really enjoyed it except Boots. She ate until her belly stuck out like a basketball. "See?" she said to Gregor, pulling up her shirt.

He poked her stomach and shook his head. "Talk about eating like a shiner!" he said. She was probably about to hit a growth spurt. At least, he hoped so.

By the time the picnic was over, everyone was dropping from fatigue. Except Boots, who'd had a nice long nap on the trip and was ready to play. They broke up guard duty into two-hour shifts. Gregor and Temp volunteered for the first watch.

Gregor dug in his backpack for something to keep his sister quiet. Since he hadn't planned to bring her along, he hadn't come prepared to entertain her. The best he could do was the binoculars.

"Look, Boots, magic glasses," he told her. He had to take a few minutes to show her how to look through the binoculars. She was fascinated by the magnified images. She peered into the eyepieces and then dropped them down repeatedly. "Temp is big. Temp is small. Temp is big. Temp is small."

"Shh. Everybody's going to sleep," said Gregor.

"Temp is big. Temp is small. Temp is big. Temp is small," whispered Boots.

Gregor was glad to get a little time with the cockroach. Temp rarely spoke in large groups, although in private he'd chatter along with Boots and Hazard in that bizarre mixture of English and Cockroach the three had developed. Most of the time, it was easy to forget Temp was there.

"So, Temp, what do you make of this thing with the nibblers?" asked Gregor when the others were asleep.

"Hate the nibblers, the rats do, hate the nibblers," said Temp.

"Well, we don't know if the rats are involved yet," said Gregor.

"It be too late, the knowing, it be," said Temp.

"Too late for what, Temp?" said Gregor.

"For the doing," said Temp.

"Doing something to help the nibblers, you mean?" asked Gregor, and the roach nodded.

By the time Gregor's watch was over, Boots had worn herself out. He lay down with her, and she soon drifted off. It took him a little longer. He kept thinking about what Temp had said, about it being too late for the doing. Gregor glanced unhappily around the empty colony, afraid that the cockroach might be right.

No one felt satisfied with the idea of returning to Regalia the next morning.

"What we have seen will not be enough to incite the council to action," said Luxa.

"Perhaps telling the story of your crown will aid our case, after all," said Howard.

"No. As Cevian was not able to tell us the reason she sent it, it will be assumed the twisters drove the nibblers out of the jungle and have gone in search of a new home," said Luxa.

"What about the marks of secret?" said Hazard. "That would be enough in the jungle."

"But we do not know specifically why they were made, so the council will not be able to justify sending soldiers after the nibblers," said Luxa.

"In truth, Cousin, I believe the most likely scenario is that the rats drove the nibblers out of both of their colonies. But we have no evidence of that. And even if we did, we have never sent an army to prevent the nibblers' relocation before," said Howard.

"We should have," said Luxa grimly.

"What about that basketful of baby mice?" said Gregor. That somehow disturbed him more than anything else.

"The council could say, like you did, that the mother was mad. Or, if something drove the nibblers out, that she did not believe the babies could make the journey. They will reason all of this away. Yet when I add it up, the crown, Cevian's death, the baby mice, two empty colonies, and the marks of secret, I know in my heart that a grievous wrong is occurring," said Luxa. "We must find more substantial proof."

"That will be hard to get, since we will all be restricted to quarters the instant we return to Regalia," said Howard.

"My mom will send Boots and me home," said Gregor. "I doubt she'll let us come back again."

"For how long?" asked Hazard.

"Maybe forever, Hazard," said Gregor. His family was only waiting for his mother's return. The second she could manage it, she'd pack them all up and take them to Virginia.

"You mean, we will not see you after this trip?" said Luxa.

"Probably not," said Gregor. It didn't seem quite real that by tomorrow he might never see the Underlanders again. But his mom would never trust him down here, especially since he'd taken Boots on this "picnic."

"We would not have allowed you to come if we knew this!" said Luxa. She was always running off on dangerous adventures, and there were never any real repercussions. But Gregor was not a queen and the Underland was not his home. "But wait, you must be wrong, Gregor. What of 'The Proph —'"

Luxa cut herself off, but Gregor could complete the phrase. What of "The Prophecy of Time"? The prophecy no one wanted to tell him about. The one about him "possibly" killing the Bane one of these days. He thought about pursuing the subject, but Nerissa had said knowledge of the prophecy might be damaging to him or people he loved. Was she afraid that if he knew what it said he'd run off and do something stupid? He remembered how obsessively he had thought about "The Prophecy of Blood" as he tried to work out its meaning . . . that hadn't helped anything . . . but the idea of this new one kept nagging at him. He decided not to ask Luxa about "The Prophecy of Time," but when he got back to Regalia he was going to confront Vikus about it. What did it say exactly? Was it definitely about Gregor? Because if it was, he would have to stay in the Underland to fulfill it, and his mom would never agree to that. For now, he would pretend he hadn't heard Luxa's comment.

"Look, me leaving . . . it was going to happen pretty soon, even if I didn't come here," said Gregor. "But I wanted to come. To help you find out what happened to the nibblers."

"Which we still do not know," said Howard. "Not what happened to them nor where they are now. They were not killed here, anyway. Nor thrown in the river, for their bodies would have washed past Regalia."

"They went deeper into the tunnels, then," said Luxa.

"Possibly," said Howard. "But how is it that a colony of nibblers escaped the notice of the Fount scouts? They patrol these regions."

"So, where could they have gone?" asked Gregor.

"I can think of only one alternative. The Swag," said Howard.

"What's that?" said Gregor.

"A tunnel that runs from these caves under the river," said Luxa. "Do you know where the entrance lies, Howard?"

"I do. I had friends among the nibblers who showed me. I have crossed the Swag once. And I cannot help feeling we may find some answers there," said Howard. "But I would not risk bringing further trouble to Gregor."

"Forget that. I've exceeded my trouble limit," said

Gregor. "Do the Swag, don't do the Swag. I'm still getting sent home."

"What harm can it do, Howard? We are all past redeeming," said Luxa.

A few minutes later, they had located the mouth of the Swag and were practically sliding down the steep slope of the tunnel. It was particularly difficult to get a footing because the floor was covered in some kind of gravel. The tunnel was large enough for the bats to fly through, but since they were hoping to find clues to the nibblers' whereabouts, they agreed that a slow journey on foot would be more helpful than a quick flight.

Crossing the Swag reminded Gregor of riding the subway that linked Manhattan to Brooklyn at 14th Street. You had to go under the East River. It was not a long trip, only a few minutes, but at about the half-way point Gregor always felt a little anxious. It was something, having a whole river running above your head. Wouldn't it have been better to build a bridge?

Eventually the slope tapered off and they were walking on even ground. For the first time, Gregor felt able to concentrate on something other than his feet. He moved his flashlight beam across the gravel floor, hoping for a sign that the nibblers had been this way, but the rocks yielded nothing. He tried examining the tunnel walls next. At first, they seemed as untouched as the gravel, but just as the floor began to turn upward, indicating they were nearing the far side of the river, Gregor spotted something.

"Wait a minute," he said. He crossed to the wall and shone his light on a spot about a foot above the floor. It was a paw print, slightly smeared but unmistakable. "Look here." He kneeled down and braced himself against the wall with one hand.

The others gathered around. "It is a nibbler print," said Luxa. "There is no doubting that. But what is it made of?"

Howard scraped the print with his fingernail, rubbed the residue between his fingers, and sniffed it. He held his hand out to Nike for confirmation. "Blood?" he said.

"Nibbler blood," she confirmed. "But a few days old."

"If you didn't have time to scratch out another scythe . . ." began Gregor.

"Or if you could not be seen doing it . . ." said Luxa.

"Right. This would be a fast way to leave a message," said Gregor.

"Especially if one was already bleeding," said Aurora.

They stood staring silently at the paw print. There was a whole story behind it. As there was in Cevian's cold body and the basket of baby nibblers and the empty colonies. In and of itself, it was not proof of anything. But Gregor's instincts told him that Luxa was right. That it all added up to something . . . evil. That was a funny word. A word for comic books and action-adventure cartoons. Not a word he ever even used in its real sense. But here in the tunnel it felt real.

Luxa, as if unable to help herself, pressed her hand on top of the paw print. Her head dropped forward slightly, and for a moment she squeezed her eyes shut tight. Gregor could almost feel the sorrow radiating from her.

He was trying to figure out what to do next when he noticed the tremor beneath his feet. "It's just another subway going by," he thought. The trains made the platforms vibrate, and you could even feel them aboveground. Then he remembered he had not arrived in this tunnel by subway.

"Mount up!" cried Howard, and the bats fluttered into positions for takeoff.

"What is it?" asked Hazard. "What is happening?"

Gregor grabbed up Boots and hurdled onto Ares's back. He did not need to wait for Howard's answer to know this was his first earthquake.

11

Gregor and Boots had just landed on Ares's back when a shock wave knocked the bat off his feet. Ares managed to get into the air, as did Nike, who carried Howard, and Aurora, who had Luxa. But Thalia was not so lucky. The little bat, with Hazard on her back, was thrown sideways.

"Hazard!" cried Luxa. She swooped down on Aurora with her arms extended to pull him up beside her, but he brushed her away.

"No, Luxa, I must stay with Thalia!" said Hazard. "We mean to be bonds!"

"She cannot take flight with you on her back!" said Howard. "Oh, we have no time for this! Nike!" Nike dove for Thalia, and Howard plucked the boy off her back with one hand.

"Thalia!" shrieked Hazard as Howard hauled him onto Nike's back. "Thalia!" Despite desperate flutterings of her wings, Thalia could not get into the air.

The entire world seemed to be shaking now, and a deep rumbling sound threatened to drown out their voices.

"Hold tight!" ordered Ares, and Gregor locked his legs around the bat and his arms around Boots as they tipped downward. Then they were level again, but Gregor could feel the drag on Ares and knew he had Thalia in his claws. "Which way?" the bat cried. "Back to the colony?"

"No, we will never make it. Follow me!" said Howard, and headed up the tunnel that led to the far side of the Swag.

Rock chips began to rain down from the roof of the tunnel. First small ones, like the gravel that lined the floor, but soon larger pieces. One caught Gregor on the shoulder, and the sharp edge cut through his shirt to his flesh. He pressed Boots forward over Ares's neck, protecting her with his body as best he could. Suddenly an awful thought hit him. "Temp! We left Temp behind!" He had not seen the cockroach on anyone's bat. A reassuring bump came from behind

Gregor, and he knew the bug must have scurried up on Ares when the earthquake started. A good thing, too, because there was no going back for a rescue.

With his head bent over Ares's neck, Gregor could see the floor, rolling as if the gravel were waves on the ocean.

Cracks began to appear in the walls of the tunnel. First thin lines, which shot up the stone faces, etching treelike patterns in the surfaces. And then deeper fissures. That's when Gregor felt the water on the back of his neck. It was only a gentle patter like rain, but he knew that wouldn't last.

"The roof! It's breaking! The river's coming in!" he cried. He didn't know if Ares could hear him over the noise. Anyway, he was already flying as well as he could. The falling rocks had increased in both size and quantity, and despite the bat's best efforts, he could not dodge them all.

Suddenly the waves of gravel were replaced by rushing water and Gregor knew that somewhere behind him the river had broken through. The mouth of the tunnel was in sight. Nike and Aurora had just shot out into freedom when the wave hit Ares.

Boots was ripped from Gregor's arms. Ares

disappeared from under him. Gregor was alone in the water, dragged along, unable even to seek air, because he had no idea where the air might be. "Boots!" his brain screamed. "Boots!"

Gregor was dashed against some rocks and allowed one ragged breath before another swell of water engulfed him. He tumbled over and over in the black water. His head struck something and he gasped, filling his lungs with water. He felt consciousness slipping away.

Then he was vaguely aware of a sharp pain in his foot and there was air around him again. He was dangling in space, water running from his nose and mouth. A bat had him from above, but he was unable to see which one.

The claw released him on a stone outcropping where he choked out the rest of the river he'd inhaled. The earth trembled ever so slightly beneath him. Gregor forced himself onto his knees. His flashlight was still working. Howard, Luxa, and Aurora lay bloody and gasping beside him. The wave must have caught them as well. There was no sign of the others.

"Boots!" Gregor cried out. His flashlight beam cut into the darkness. They were up very high over an expanse of churning water. Several hundred yards away, he could just see the top of what must have been the opening to the Swag. Ares and Nike were speeding over the water, searching for the others.

"Hazard! Hazard!" Luxa's voice was as desperate as his own.

Boots, Hazard, Thalia, Temp. The smallest, the youngest, the most vulnerable, were all missing.

"Aurora, can you fly? Can you fly?" begged Luxa. But the golden bat was still gagging up water and unable to answer.

The flashlight beam caught something floundering in a shallow area nearby. Ares dove and when he came up he had a sodden Thalia in his claws. And in her claws was Hazard.

Ares gently laid the pair on the stone before he fluttered off again. Thalia was waterlogged, probably going into shock, but she was at least still fighting. Hazard appeared lifeless. His pale skin had a bluish tint. Blood ran from a deep gash in his forehead. There was no movement in his chest.

Howard was over the boy at once, trying to restore his breathing. It took both Gregor and Aurora, who had recovered slightly, to hold Luxa back from Hazard.

"Let Howard do it! He's an expert!" Gregor said as she struggled. If Mareth were here, he'd have just knocked Luxa out. He'd done that to Howard when he'd flipped out the time his bat, Pandora, had been devoured by mites. But Gregor couldn't imagine hitting Luxa that hard.

When she'd calmed down enough that Aurora could contain her, Gregor waved his arms and called to Ares to retrieve him. They flew low over the water, searching frantically for a sign of life.

"Boots!" yelled Gregor. "Boots!" Every second that passed drained another bit of hope from his heart.

He could feel despair overtaking him when a tiny wail caught his ear. "Ma-maa!" It increased in volume. "Ma-maa!"

"Oh, man, she's alive!" said Gregor as tears of relief blurred his vision. "Boots! I'm coming! Hang on!"

"Ma-maa!" came back at him, but they still couldn't find her.

"Where is she, Ares?" said Gregor.

"I do not know! I cannot locate her!" said his bat.

"Ma-maa!" The cry was fainter this time.

Gregor felt the darkness was about to swallow her up forever. "Boots! Where are you?" As if she could tell him. But it turned out she could. For suddenly a pinprick of light caught his eye. Her scepter! Her stupid, silly, wonderful, amazing, and apparently waterproof princess scepter!

They found her in a small pool. Weeping. Her tiara and princess skirt gone. Clutching her scepter. Sitting on Temp's back as he paddled around in a circle, unable to climb up the steep rocks that surrounded them.

"Oh, sweetie," said Gregor as he pulled her up into his arms. "Oh, Boots."

She clung to him but was mad at him, too. "You let go. In the water. You let go of me!" she sobbed, and hit him with her small fist.

"I'm sorry. I tried not to. I'm sorry, Boots," he said, but she was not ready to forgive him.

There was no easy way to retrieve Temp. Ares ended up tossing the cockroach into the air with his snout and catching him on his back. Temp landed with a hollow thud that couldn't have felt too good, but the bug wasn't one to complain.

Boots, on the other hand, was just warming up. "You let Temp go! You let Temp go, too!"

"I'm sorry. I'm sorry," was all Gregor could say as they coasted in to join the others.

Howard was still trying to restore Hazard's breathing when the earth began to shake again.

"An aftershock," thought Gregor. "I think that's what they're called." As he locked his arms around Boots he wondered if they should be trying to escape. But where do you run to when the whole world is unstable?

The sharp collision of rock on rock drew Gregor's attention back to the exit of the Swag. The stone wall above the tunnel, already cracked and damaged from the initial earthquake, began to break away. A deafening explosion of sound assaulted his ears, and then he was lying on his side, Boots still in his arms.

He lifted the flashlight just in time to see the avalanche bury the opening to the Swag under a mountain of rock.

CHAPTER
12

The impact of the avalanche as it hit the water was enough to send waves splashing over the edge of their haven, but no one was washed away. Nor could anyone get any wetter. They were all soaked, inside and out.

Howard was almost oblivious to the latest disaster, because he was so focused on Hazard. The rest of them sat dripping and shivering as he pumped the boy's chest and gave him mouth-to-mouth resuscitation. The seconds dragged on. Luxa had stopped fighting and now just stared at Hazard, stiff and distant. Gregor knew she thought the boy was lost.

Only when Howard cried out, "His heart beats!" did everyone come to life.

Luxa sprang forward and clutched Hazard's hand, saying, "He is alive? He is alive?"

At that moment, water gushed from Hazard's mouth. Howard rolled the boy on his side and let Luxa comfort him as he retched. The picnic hampers were still secured to the bats' backs. Howard dug into the smaller hamper on Nike and pulled out a large leather box. Leave it to Howard to think to pack a first-aid kit. It had never even crossed Gregor's mind. Just another reason he was probably not doctor material.

Gregor had brought flashlights, though, and several spare batteries, which was good because, besides Boots's scepter, that was all the light he had. The torches had been taken by the flood.

"I must stitch his wound," said Howard. While Luxa cradled Hazard in her arms, Howard cleaned and sewed up the gash in his forehead with quick, deft strokes. He shone Gregor's flashlight in Hazard's eyes and checked his pupils.

"Will he recover?" asked Luxa.

"Oh, yes. Just a knock on the head and a bit too much water," said Howard cheerfully. "Next time you are thirsty, Hazard, you might try a cup instead of a river."

Hazard managed a weak smile. "I will."

Thalia laughed hysterically until she began to cry. The whole day had been too much for Thalia. Nike snuggled the little bat in her wings until she could calm down.

Howard stripped off Hazard's wet clothes and wrapped him in a blanket. "I will wager your head aches." Howard gave Hazard a swallow from a big green bottle that Gregor recognized as painkiller. "Try and lie still. Can you do that?" Hazard gave a nod.

"All right, then. How fare the rest of you?" said Howard.

They all just stared at him. Their injuries so paled in comparison to Hazard's that no one felt they could complain. Except for Boots, of course.

"Gre-go let me go," she said, still sniffling. "Look." She held up her little pointer finger dramatically. It would have been an exaggeration to call it a cut. A nick maybe.

"Oh, dear. We must address that immediately," said Howard. "And line up, all of you. I do not want anyone being brave."

It took less than a minute to fix up Boots, and then Howard worked his way through the rest of the party, stitching up cuts and checking for broken bones. They were banged up and bruised, but no one had serious injuries. Luxa, who had been holding Hazard while the others were treated, came up last. She had sprained a finger on her left hand.

While Howard immobilized it with a thin strip of stone and fabric, she said, "I am so grateful you came."

"I would like that to be carved in stone. For when you are deciding who to invite on future picnics," said Howard.

"Thank you for saving Hazard," said Luxa tremulously.

"He is my cousin," said Howard as he tied off the fabric. "As are you, right?"

In answer, Luxa put her arms around Howard's neck. "Oh, no, are you actually giving me a hug?" He hugged her back, grinning at Gregor over her shoulder. "And it only took an earthquake, a flood, and an avalanche to get it."

They all laughed then, even the bats and Temp. Even Luxa.

Now that the immediate crisis was over, they had to deal with the larger crisis at hand.

"The avalanche blocked the Swag. So, how do we

get back to Regalia?" asked Gregor. The pursuit of the mice was over. They had to get Hazard home now.

"It is easier said than done," said Howard. "For we are in Hades Hall."

"Okay, what's that?" asked Gregor.

"It is a long passageway that goes very deep into the earth. But there are only two ways to gain entrance to it. On this end, the Swag, which is no longer an option. At the far end, many miles from here, the Firelands," said Howard.

"What, there's no other way to get out?" asked Gregor.

"I am afraid not. There are some caves. But no other tunnels," said Howard.

"The Firelands . . . aren't they near the jungle?" asked Gregor. He was trying to call up the image of the Underland map he had once seen, but it was foggy.

"Yes. The journey should require about five days of travel. Three for Hades Hall, and two to get back to Regalia. But before we begin, we must eat; we must rest. We are all in need of recovery, and I would not move Hazard so soon," said Howard.

No one wanted to eat. The river water had made their stomachs feel weird. Gregor put his flashlight on low and set it in the middle of the group. It was all they could allow themselves, with a long trip ahead and no torches.

"Your light, Gregor. How long will it last?" asked Luxa.

"Not for five days," said Gregor.

"I don't like the dark," said Hazard plaintively. "I miss the jungle. There was always some light there."

"When we sleep, Hazard, it will not matter if it is light or dark," said Luxa, smoothing back his curls. "May he go to sleep now, Howard?"

"Yes, Hazard may rest, but we must wake him every time the watch changes," said Howard. "It is standard with head injuries."

Luxa wanted the first watch. She was still too worried about Hazard to do anything else. Gregor realized that her loving Hazard had brought a new dimension of anxiety into her life. Made her vulnerable in a way she had not been before. It was unbearable to think about losing anyone you loved, but that time Gregor had thought he'd lost Boots it was as if the world had ended. Little kids . . . you just loved them in a special way.

Between the incident with Hazard and her ongoing fear for the mice, Luxa was being pushed to the limit.

Gregor volunteered to take the watch with her before anyone else had a chance. Just to keep an eye on her.

Despite the dampness of their clothes and fur and even Temp's shell — periodically trickles of water would run out of some part of him — the others fell asleep quickly.

Gregor sat next to Luxa on the smaller picnic hamper that she had positioned over Hazard's bedside. He reviewed his situation in his head.

Boy, was he ever in trouble now. The list of his transgressions was quite impressive. He had secretly gone to the mouse colony with Luxa. He had taken Boots along. He had crossed the Swag, which he knew nothing about, and then been cut off by an avalanche. He was five days from reaching Regalia, which meant during that time his family would be in hell. All they would know was that he had taken Boots on a picnic and never returned. A thought hit him.

"Hey, Luxa, if all that water ran into the Swag from the river, they would know in Regalia, right? I mean, the whole river would be lower," said Gregor.

"Yes, I suppose so. The water here stopped rising after the avalanche. It seemed to have blocked it off. But we have no idea what happened on the other side of the Swag," said Luxa. "Why?"

"I was thinking, at least people might guess we had come here and know it might take us some time to get home," said Gregor. "I mean, say they came to investigate why the river was low. And they found where we'd had a fire at the nibblers' colony. Maybe they could put two and two together and know we'd gone through the Swag."

"But, Gregor, that could have been anyone's fire. And once the river fills the Swag it may flood the nibblers' colony as well, erasing all signs of us," said Luxa.

She was right. If a big wave had come out of this side of the Swag, a big wave had probably come out of the other side, too. Gregor didn't know enough about science to even guess what would happen to the river or to the surrounding areas when everything had settled.

"Besides, they have no reason to think we would come so far. Had it been only you and I, possibly. We are not much trusted. But we took Hazard and Boots, whom we cherish. And Howard . . . no one ever would expect Howard to make such an unauthorized trip. He is so dependably good," said Luxa.

"That didn't keep them from putting him on trial for treason," said Gregor.

"True enough, but he was easily cleared of the

charge. And this morning Vikus saw us off with two hampers of food. I expect they are searching well-frequented picnic sites for us," said Luxa.

"Oh. It was just a thought," said Gregor. "So . . . how are you doing?"

"Better, now that Hazard breathes," said Luxa.

"Don't worry. Howard will make sure he's okay," said Gregor.

"Yes, Howard watches over him," said Luxa.

"He watches over you, too," said Gregor, remembering his uncomfortable date conversation. His face turned hot again. "Look, you know when we were leaving Regalia and I said that whole thing about the picnic being a date? I'm sorry. That was just to get us out of there. I didn't mean . . . you see, I didn't know . . . in the Overland a date's not that big a deal . . . well, it would be for me, but for other people . . . okay, you can stop staring at me now. I'm done."

Those violet eyes had been locked on his face as he floundered through the explanation. "Did Howard say something to you about it?" asked Luxa, not looking away.

"Yeah. He made it pretty clear you and I weren't going on any dates," said Gregor.

They both laughed.

"I knew you did not mean anything by it," said Luxa. "I am sure I am not at all the person you would choose to invite on a date."

"That's not true," Gregor blurted out. Oh, man! Why did he say that? She had been perfectly willing to go with the "that was just to get us out of Regalia" excuse! And here he was, stepping right back into it. "I mean, there's nothing wrong with you." That sounded bad, too. "It's just the whole queen thing."

"And the Overlander thing," she said, finally looking away.

"Yeah," he said. What did that mean? That if he weren't an Overlander she might . . . she might what? He had to stop this now. He needed to change the subject. New subject . . . new subject . . . "Do you want a sandwich?" he said.

"A sandwich?" said Luxa. "Yes."

"I'll make some," said Gregor. They ate cheese sandwiches and talked very little. When Ares and Nike awoke to take the next shift, Gregor lay down next to Boots and pulled the edge of the blanket up over his face, grateful to be away from Luxa's eyes.

The next morning, while they had breakfast,

Howard explained the geography of Hades Hall. "I have never traveled it myself. Humans rarely take this route, for others are shorter and less perilous."

"Where does it come out exactly?" asked Gregor.

"In the Firelands. Here, Gregor, it is like this," said Howard. He dipped his finger in some kind of spicy sauce and drew an *A*. "We are here." To the left of the *A* he made a long line. "Here is the river that leads into the Waterway." A large oval indicated the Waterway. To the left of the Waterway, way off to the side, he made a *B*. "Here lie the Firelands. And Hades Hall runs something like this." Howard drew an *S*-shaped line between points *A* and *B*.

Gregor stared at the map. Something was confusing him. "Where's Regalia?"

"Here," said Howard, indicating a point directly on top of the *S*-shaped line.

"So, why don't we run into Regalia on the way?" said Gregor.

"Because Hades Hall is far below Regalia and there is no access to it. You must not think of the Underland as a flat plain. Think of it as a sphere, where one can go up and down as well as side to side," said Howard.

"At one point, Regalia will be directly over our

heads," said Luxa. "I do not much like going so deep in the earth." Which Gregor found ironic, since she already lived miles below the planet's surface.

They packed up their gear and got ready to travel. Hazard was the greatest concern. Howard settled him on Aurora's back, giving Luxa specific instructions for his care. Gregor took Boots and Temp on Ares, Howard rode Nike, and they all just hoped that Thalia, without a rider, might be able to keep up.

At first Gregor was optimistic. Hades Hall was a massive tunnel. At times he could not see both sides of it at once. It had clean streams filled with fish, so they weren't likely to dehydrate or starve. The floor was rocky and uneven, but they would be up on the bats. On the whole, it seemed like it would be a decent enough trip.

As the hours passed, though, he felt they were making little headway. The tunnel began to slope so dramatically that at times the bats were practically free-falling in space. They couldn't really fly . . . they just sort of dropped and occasionally opened their wings to guide themselves. It was not a speedy way to travel. Besides that, it seemed like they were stopping every ten minutes for something. Boots had to pee;

Thalia needed a break; Hazard's bandage had to be changed; Nike spotted a good stream and thought they should fill their water skins as a precaution.

They carried on this way for about six hours, until Howard said they would have to make camp for the night. Hazard couldn't travel anymore. Hades Hall was still angled sharply down, but they found a big ledge on the tunnel wall to stay on.

Hazard and the bats went to sleep. The rest of them gathered around the beam of Gregor's flashlight and tried to act like they weren't worried. Well, Boots really wasn't worried. She played I Spy with Temp. It wasn't much of a game, since it was too dark to see stuff. But that didn't stop her.

"I spy, with my little eye, something that is black!" she said about a thousand times. Temp would try to guess. Often the big reveal was just Boots pointing into the darkness at different angles and saying, "That!"

They were all a little relieved when she finally fell asleep. Gregor felt free to bring up something that had been weighing on him since that morning. Something he had not wanted to discuss in front of the little kids. "Howard, you said this trip was more perilous than other routes. What did you mean by that exactly?"

"The depth of the tunnels is difficult to navigate. The air becomes foul as we near the Firelands. And then there are creatures who live here who would rather not be disturbed," said Howard.

"Dangerous creatures?" asked Gregor.

"Some. Most will simply avoid us. Of those who would seek to do us harm, many do not fly, so we shall elude them. And then there are others who are not hostile but must be acknowledged," said Howard.

"Like who?" said Gregor.

It was as if the creature in the darkness had only been waiting for the right opportunity to break in. And when he spoke, Gregor recognized the high whiny voice immediately. How could he forget it?

"Greetings, all! I am he called Photos Glow-Glow . . . and she is Zap."

13

"No way!" was the first thing that burst out of Gregor's mouth. He had never expected to see the fireflies again. The bugs had deserted the ship on the quest to find the Bane and betrayed everyone aboard to the rats. Gregor, Boots, Ares, Howard, Luxa, Aurora, and Temp had all nearly been killed because of their deception. Gregor didn't know what the fireflies were doing here in Hades Hall, but he couldn't believe that they had the guts to come up with a big friendly hello.

Howard, who had been the most outraged at the bugs' disloyalty, sprang to his feet and drew his sword. "Show yourselves, shiners!" he shouted into the darkness, waking the bats. "Show yourselves, you bloated bags of treachery!"

There was a long pause. Then Gregor heard Zap say, "Well, that was rude."

"Very rude," agreed Photos Glow-Glow.

"And after all we did for them. One would think a little gratitude might be in order," said Zap in a wounded tone.

"Gratitude!" spat out Howard. "You sold us to the rats and now you expect gratitude? Show yourselves!"

"Someone has a very selective memory," said Photos Glow-Glow. "You do not seem to recall how we starved for you, guided you across the Waterway, and masterfully defended you from the squid!"

"I remember you ate some squid," said Gregor. "That's about it." He hadn't even bothered to rise. The shiners were such lazy, inept creatures, he knew they would never attack. He supposed he could chase them down in the dark . . . and then what? He despised them, but he wasn't going to go kill them.

But Howard was of another mind. "Nike!" he called. "Let us rid ourselves of these traitors once and for all!" Nike fluttered to his side.

It was Luxa who grabbed Howard by the arm. "Wait," she said.

Howard looked at her in surprise. "Do you not join me, Cousin? After all you have suffered at their hands?"

Gregor could barely hear the next thing she whispered to Howard. "They have light."

Howard's shoulders hunched forward as he wrestled with what she was suggesting. Finally, he shoved his sword back in his belt.

"Shiners, will you not show yourselves?" said Luxa pleasantly. "We mean you no harm."

"It seems more prudent to remain aloof," said Photos Glow-Glow.

"He means aloft," said Zap. "He can never keep words straight."

"I meant aloof! As in distant, remote, and detached!" said Photos Glow-Glow.

And the two launched into a big argument about "aloof" and "aloft." When they were winded, Luxa tried again.

"That is too bad. For we find ourselves with an overabundance of food that will soon be unfit to eat. Particularly cake," she said.

"Cake?" said Zap. There was another long pause.

"Has this cake . . . been frosted?" asked Photos Glow-Glow.

"Oh, yes. I do not care for it any other way," said Luxa. "But it is such a pity to waste it." She removed a round cake from the hamper and looked at it regretfully. It was rather battered from being tossed over and over in the flood, but it gave off a delicious smell.

"Well, Your Highness has not been rude to us, as some have. So if my eating that cake would please you . . . I do not have any objection to it," said Photos Glow-Glow.

"Nor I!" said Zap, and suddenly the pair of fireflies were right in front of Luxa, their rear ends ablaze with yellow light.

For the first time in days, Gregor could see properly. He was immediately aware of things he had missed. That there were large patches of mushrooms growing on the ceiling. That puffs of vapor periodically emerged from cracks in the walls. That Boots had a big bruise on her arm. If he had not seen these things, what else had he been blinded to? What dangers lay out in the dark beyond his vision's reach?

Gregor knew Luxa absolutely loathed the shiners. She also knew they could be of use. He had to admire how quickly she'd assessed the situation and made the decision to make peace with them. He thought Ripred would have applauded her shrewdness. It was something the big rat would have done himself. If he were here. Instead of hunting down the Bane. Or whatever. Hopefully by the time they returned to Regalia, Ripred would have checked in.

Luxa divided the cake in two and the bugs gobbled it down to the last crumb.

"How come you to be in Hades Hall, Most Gracious Queen?" said Photos Glow-Glow.

"We crossed the Swag for a lark and were cut off by an avalanche. Now we must proceed home this way," said Luxa. "And yourselves?"

"We live here," said Zap unhappily.

"You live here?" asked Gregor. He had never thought of the fireflies as living anywhere.

"We were driven out of finer lands by villains who greatly outnumbered us," said Photos Glow-Glow. "The slimers."

Howard gave a snort of derision. "Snails, Gregor. They were chased out of their lands by snails."

"Are snails fast down here?" asked Gregor.

"Fast enough!" snapped Photos Glow-Glow.

"At full speed, they travel one yard an hour," said Nike.

"But they are persistent!" said Zap indignantly.

"It is widely believed that the snails did not even know they overthrew the shiners, so nonexistent was the resistance," said Howard.

Gregor could tell Howard had hit a nerve. Zap's light came in short, angry bursts, and Photos Glow-Glow's butt had turned bright red.

"Howard, Nike, why do you provoke my guests?" said Luxa.

"We are hoping they will be offended enough to leave," said Nike.

"And I am hoping they may join us for a few days," said Luxa. "After all, this is their territory. They know it well. Do you two?"

"No," said Howard sullenly.

"Then counter not my desires," said Luxa.

"I hope you know what you are doing, Your Highness," said Howard.

"You seem tired. Why do you not get some rest?" said Luxa.

Grumbling to himself, Howard wrapped up in a blanket and lay down. Nike fluttered over to his side. They would make good bonds, Howard and Nike. They both were honorable, brave, and good-natured. Already they trusted each other with their secrets. And they clearly agreed about the shiners.

"It seems that some believe us to be the villains in our last encounter. When in truth it was you humans who broke your contract with us," said Photos Glow-Glow. "We were guaranteed a certain measure of food . . . which was not supplied."

"We stayed extra days, just as a favor," said Zap.

"Yes, unquestionably we were the injured party," said Photos Glow-Glow.

It was sort of interesting to hear things from the fireflies' perspective. They had some valid points, in a way. The trip to find the Bane hadn't been their quest. They were hired lightbulbs. Gregor still couldn't stand them, though.

"It wasn't so much that you left. It's that you told the rats we were coming," said Gregor.

The fireflies shifted around uncomfortably.

"That was Zap's idea," mumbled Photos Glow-Glow.

"Liar!" shrieked Zap. She flew furiously at Photos Glow-Glow.

Their heads smacked into each other with an unpleasant cracking sound, and they both plopped back on the ground, groaning and spitting insults at each other. Then they just glowered at each other.

"Well, let us let bygones be bygones," said Luxa. "Perhaps you will journey with us through Hades Hall. I cannot promise large quantities of food, but we will share what we have and the fliers are excellent fishers."

Photos Glow-Glow and Zap agreed, probably because they were hoping for more cake. Besides, what else did they have to do? Gregor couldn't imagine them having enough willpower to work up any constructive plan for themselves. If their species had been driven out of their lands by snails, they weren't highly motivated. They made it seem like their schedule was packed, though.

"Well, I suppose we can fit it in," said Zap. "If we break a few other commitments."

"Yes, others will be disappointed, but we will fit it in," said Photos Glow-Glow. "We can hardly leave you down here with the rats to fend for yourselves."

"Rats?" said Howard, sitting right up. He hadn't been sleeping at all. "Have you seen gnawers down here of late?"

"Oh, look who deigns to speak to us now," said Photos Glow-Glow.

"Yes, la-de-da-da," agreed Zap.

"Shiners, if you have knowledge of the gnawers, I would greatly appreciate your sharing it," said Luxa.

"They came past our lands," said Zap, indicating the tunnel ahead of them with a nod.

"After the nibblers," said Photos Glow-Glow.

All that had happened, the earthquake, the flood, the avalanche, Hazard's injury, and the journey through Hades Hall, had overshadowed the nibblers' plight for Gregor. But he could tell by Luxa's response that she had never stopped thinking of them.

"Where?" she said, springing to her feet. "How many nibblers? Were the rats with them or did they flee? Tell me!"

"Oh, there must have been hundreds," said Zap. "Maybe thousands."

"The rats were driving them somewhere. They are always driving the nibblers somewhere. Out of the caves, into the jungle, out of the jungle, into the tunnels. The whole thing is very tedious to watch," said Photos Glow-Glow.

"We fell asleep," said Zap.

"Were these nibblers from the jungle?" asked Gregor.

"No, they took the ones from the jungle straight to the Firelands," said Zap. "At least, I think someone said that. It was days ago. But the rats have been moving the nibblers around for years."

"Maybe they'll just leave them all in the Firelands and stop annoying the rest of us," said Photos Glow-Glow.

"The nibblers could not make a decent home in the Firelands," said Nike.

"Everyone has troubles, and no one helps," said Zap. "Look at us. Those slimers drove us from our home, and who came to our aid?"

"No one knew you were under attack," said Luxa.

"Because . . . we were too proud to ask for help!" said Photos Glow-Glow dramatically.

"And it was such a long trip to Regalia," admitted Zap. "Nobody wanted to fly that far."

"But mostly . . . because we were too proud to ask for help!" repeated Photos Glow-Glow with a flourish.

The fireflies claimed they'd flown for hours and had to be exempted from watch duty that night. Soon they were snoring.

Luxa asked Howard to take the first shift with her, and as he drifted off to sleep Gregor could hear her trying to reason with her cousin about the shiners, saying they would give Hazard comfort and that they might reveal more information about the nibblers.

The next morning, Gregor was awakened by Boots's surprised voice. "Fo-Fo? Are you Fo-Fo?"

"I am he called Photos Glow-Glow and will answer to no other name!" said the firefly.

"Oh, shiners!" said Hazard, rubbing his eyes and smiling. "How bright they are!"

"Temp! Temp! Look! Fo-Fo is here!" said Boots cheerfully.

"I said, I am he called . . . oh, never mind," said Photos Glow-Glow crankily.

His mood improved with breakfast. The bats fished to provide a base for the fireflies' meal, and Luxa gave them each some shrimp salad. It was starting to spoil, but they didn't seem to notice.

The little band hadn't flown for five minutes when they passed the fireflies' current home. It was an enormous cave off Hades Hall that emitted a continuous whiny buzz. Multicolored lights flashed from the inhabitants' butts and a few voices demanded to know what

179

Photos Glow-Glow and Zap were doing, but none of the other bugs could be bothered to fly out and find out.

Apparently Photos Glow-Glow and Zap were real go-getters for their species.

Hades Hall continued to veer downward at an alarming rate. They were moving deeper into the earth every moment. Often when Gregor swallowed his ears would pop.

They had to stop many times and fish for the fireflies just to keep the bugs going. Gregor wondered if they were really worth the effort. Then he remembered being knocked around the cave by Twirltongue and her friends and knew that they were.

"We near the bottom," said Photos Glow-Glow finally.

"Good, we will make camp there," said Howard.

"Not us," said Zap.

"Why not?" asked Gregor.

"Are your noses of no use at all?" asked Photos Glow-Glow.

There was a smell. A horrendous smell, wafting up from below them. Gregor flashed back to a summer several years ago, the farm in Virginia, his grandpa dragging a possum carcass from under the shed. "Something died down there," Gregor thought. A moment later, he saw them.

At least a hundred mice lay twisted and motionless at the bottom of the tunnel.

CHAPTER

14

"The mouses take a nap?" said Boots.

"Kill the lights!" Gregor shouted at the fireflies. In another few seconds even Boots would realize that the mice were not sleeping but dead. Some lay in pools of dried blood. The eyes of others were wide open as they stared frozen into space. "Turn them off!"

The bulbs on Photos Glow-Glow's and Zap's rear ends went dark. Gregor flicked on the flashlight at his belt but did not direct it to the ground.

"What did Boots say? What mice? Did we find the nibblers?" asked Hazard, struggling to sit up.

"Lie back, Hazard; there is nothing to see," said Howard.

"What is that smell?" Hazard insisted.

"It comes from a foul stream. We will fly on," said Luxa.

None of them wanted Hazard or Boots to see the corpses. But there was no concealing them from Thalia. When they found a place to land about a thousand yards beyond the graveyard, Gregor noticed the little bat was trembling. He felt pretty shaky himself.

Howard made a bed for Hazard and then pulled Luxa and Gregor aside. "One of us must stay with the young ones while the other two go back."

"I must go," said Luxa.

"You stay, Howard. In case Hazard feels bad or something," said Gregor.

They left Howard, Nike, and Temp to watch over Hazard, Boots, and Thalia. Photos Glow-Glow stayed at the campsite while Zap escorted Gregor and Luxa and their bonds back to the mice.

Before they left, Howard provided them with cloths wetted with an antiseptic solution to hold over their noses as a barrier to the smell of decomposing flesh. "Do not touch any of them," he instructed. "You do not know what contagion they might carry."

The cloths helped, but when they reached the mice Gregor still could not help gagging at the stench.

Zap's light was enough to illuminate the whole area. The bottom of the tunnel had ended with a sheer drop of about forty feet. The mice must have been driven straight off the side of the cliff and fallen to their deaths. Some, by their squashed and battered appearance, had clearly broken the fall of others. Several pups were crushed completely. There were no rats among the dead.

Even Zap, who showed remarkably little compassion in general, seemed affected by the scene. "What a waste. What a waste. I do not pretend to like the nibblers, but what a waste."

"I guess they ran right off the edge of the cliff," said Gregor.

"They would have found a way to scale the wall, had they been given time," replied Luxa bitterly. "This was the gnawers' work."

"Should we do something with the bodies?' asked Gregor.

"There is nothing to be done. If we place them in the water, we pollute our own drinking supply. We do not have enough hands to bury them in stone, nor the fuel to burn them properly," said Luxa.

All this was true. Yet somehow they couldn't just fly away and do nothing.

"We should leave something, a headstone or some message," said Gregor. But writing in stone was no small matter. He had intended to write a few sentences about what happened, but it was an effort even to scratch one straight line into the side of the cliff with his sword. As he stood considering the wall, waiting for inspiration, Luxa came up and added the thin, beaklike appendage that turned the line into the scythe. Into a mark of secret.

"It will be a warning to any that follow us," she said. "And it will be a fitting marker for the nibblers' graves."

And then Luxa did something that made Gregor feel both remarkably close to and a million miles away from her. Flinging away the cloth from her nose, she kneeled on the ground and placed her crown in front of her. Crossing her wrists, she held her hands, palms down, over the gold circle, and said in a loud voice:

"UPON THIS CROWN MY PLEDGE I GIVE.
TO MY LAST BREATH, I HOLD THIS CHOICE.

I WILL YOUR UNJUST DEATHS AVENGE,
ALL HERE WHO DIED WITHOUT A VOICE."

The words reverberated around the tunnel. It was not an impromptu rhyme, something she had made up off the top of her head. There was a specific ritual and a grim, formal tone to the lines. Gregor was certain it was an oath. Something you swore to fulfill or died trying to. It came from such an agonized place within Luxa that Gregor wanted to wrap his arms around her. But the oath had pushed him away from her, too. Had reminded him that he was just a visitor in a strange land where people vowed vengeance and crowns mattered and queens were off-limits to him.

Watching her rise, Gregor could no longer see Luxa the twelve-year-old girl who'd been searching for clues about her mouse friends. What he saw was the future head of Regalia, and its considerable armies, and that the rats were somehow going to pay with their blood.

Something was happening in the tunnel. Faint whispering sounds, buzzes, a rustle of wings. Gregor remembered what Howard had said, about how a lot of creatures lived in Hades Hall. They had been keeping a low profile so far, but they were around, watching, listening, and now reacting to Luxa's little speech. She heard the reaction and for some reason that Gregor didn't understand, she smiled.

The moan startled them. Zap brightened her beam and they saw a slight movement in the field of stillness. The tip of a tail shuddered. Disregarding Howard's warning about touching the creatures, Luxa raced to the mouse's side and crouched beside him, stroking his fur. He could not speak.

"Let's get him to Howard," said Gregor. Together, he and Luxa loaded the mouse onto Ares's back. Gregor tossed his leg over his bat's neck, but Luxa remained on the ground. "Aren't you coming?" he asked.

"No, Gregor. We will stay and make sure no others still have light," said Luxa. In the Underland, the word "light" could be interchangeable with the word "life."

Gregor looked at the victims. "We'll come back and help," he said.

"You do not have to," said Luxa. "Aurora and I can manage."

"We will come back," Ares said.

Gregor and Ares delivered the barely conscious mouse

to Howard and returned to the base of the cliff. One by one, they checked each body. Some were obviously dead. Some it was impossible to tell, so they felt for a pulse or listened for a whiff of breath coming from their nostrils. There were no other survivors.

Back at the campsite, Gregor scrubbed himself at a nearby stream, but he could not seem to get the smell of the dead mice from his pores. And the images of those bodies . . . well, he knew those would revisit him for a long time in his dreams.

Howard worked long and hard over the injured mouse. One of his front legs was broken, so Howard set the fracture. He put a salve on the mouse's raw and bloody paws. After about an hour of periodically getting him to take spoonfuls of water, Howard made a thin gruel of fish, bread crumbs, and broth and got the mouse to eat a little. The water and food revived him enough for him to speak a few words, starting with his name, Cartesian. Howard was able to ascertain the extent of Cartesian's injuries better now. The mouse had badly bruised ribs, although they did not seem broken. He'd received a blow to the head. Dehydration and hunger had also taken their toll. It was not enough information to find out exactly what had happened to

Cartesian, but it was enough to treat him. Howard made a poultice for Cartesian's head, gave him some painkiller and a second medicine to reduce swelling, and continued to feed him.

Boots wanted very badly to help, so Howard gave her the job of singing the mouse to sleep. She squatted down a few feet away and softly sang little tunes she knew from home. These were mostly theme songs from preschool shows she watched on TV. Then she launched into her Underland repertoire, which included the songs about the spinners, and the fish, and the bats.

"BAT, BAT,

COME UNDER MY HAT,

I WILL GIVE YOU A SLICE OF BACON

AND WHEN I BAKE, I WILL GIVE YOU A CAKE,

IF I AM NOT MISTAKEN."

Then she sang the stanza from the one about the queen and the nibblers and pouring tea, because she thought, as a mouse, Cartesian would like it best.

"CATCH THE NIBBLERS IN A TRAP.

WATCH THE NIBBLERS SPIN AND SNAP.

QUIET WHILE THEY TAKE A NAP.
FATHER, MOTHER, SISTER, BROTHER,
OFF THEY GO. I DO NOT KNOW
IF WE WILL SEE ANOTHER."

Cartesian slowly drifted off to sleep, and Howard praised Boots for her excellent singing job. Enamored with her newfound talent, Boots went around to everybody trying to sing them to sleep. Half the party were so tired they genuinely fell asleep; the other half pretended until Boots dozed off herself. Then Gregor, Luxa, Howard, Aurora, Nike, and Ares gathered for a consultation in the glow of Photos Glow-Glow's bulb.

"Well, as tragic as our findings today have been, at least we know we have kept to the nibblers' trail," said Howard.

"It is not much to our credit," said Luxa. "We chose this path because it was the only way out. We can be sure that we follow them to the far side of Hades Hall."

"And then?" asked Gregor.

"And then what?" asked Luxa.

"And then you're going to keep following them, aren't you? Instead of going back to Regalia," said

Gregor. She didn't answer, but he knew he was right. She wasn't going home. Not after she'd kneeled on the ground and said that stuff over the crown.

"We cannot do that. We have injured who must be returned home," said Howard. "And I believe there is enough evidence to make a case before the council, now that we have Cartesian for a witness."

"The rest of you will go back. Aurora and I will continue after the nibblers," said Luxa. "Someone must stay on their trail."

"But it will not be you, Cousin. I will drag you back to Regalia before I would leave you here alone," said Howard.

"She made some kind of oath," said Gregor. "Back at the cliff."

"Oath?" Howard looked at Luxa and his face fell. "Not 'The Vow to the Dead'?" he said in a hushed voice. Luxa nodded. "Oh, Luxa, what have you done? You are not even of age. You do not reign. The army does not move at your command. How mean you to fulfill it?"

"The only way I can," said Luxa. "I will go after the nibblers, and the council will send the army after me."

"They didn't send an army when you got caught in that rat maze," said Gregor.

"Because they thought she was dead," said Howard. "They will now. They must. Especially if she has said the vow."

"How will they even know?" said Gregor. "It's not like the humans have scouts in Hades Hall."

"Do you think only human ears matter?" scoffed Photos Glow-Glow. "The fliers heard her; that nibbler heard her; Zap heard her and has already told me. You are in Hades Hall, not the Dead Land. Who knows how many other creatures sat in the dark listening?"

"A lot," thought Gregor, remembering the strange noises that had followed Luxa's vow. That's why she had smiled. She had wanted them to hear.

"Half the Underland will know she said it in a matter of hours; she cannot take it back," said Howard.

"Nor would I if I could," said Luxa.

"But you're only, like, twelve," said Gregor. "Does it even count?"

"In this case, it counts," said Howard. "By the time word of the vow reaches the council it will already have reached our enemies. There will be no way to call it back or deny it. And given the circumstances, we will have only one option."

"What's that?" said Gregor.

Luxa gazed at him evenly. "I have just declared war on the rats."

CHAPTER
15

"So this is how a war starts," thought Gregor. Not with two armies facing off, waiting for the signal to charge. Not with a wave of rats invading the avenues of Regalia. Not with a formation of bats swooping down on an unsuspecting colony of rats. It begins much more quietly. In a room, on a field, in a remote tunnel when someone who has power decides the time has come.

"No," he said. "We have to find some way to stop it."

"It is too late," said Luxa. "It is ironic. I could never start a war in Regalia. I can barely get leave to go on a picnic. But here, away from my city, I am free to make momentous decisions."

"Then maybe they should keep you locked up in your city, if you're going to go around declaring war!" said Gregor.

"Did you not see the bodies?" exclaimed Luxa. "What would you have me do, Gregor? Sit by while my friends are driven to their death?"

"We do not know exactly what plans the gnawers have for the nibblers, Cousin," said Howard. "But we do know they have a history of moving them from place to place. Perhaps the majority of the nibblers have already reached their new home in safety."

"That they were forced from their old home is not acceptable!" said Luxa. "That hundreds lie dead from the journey is not acceptable!"

"Okay! But maybe you might want to consider some other options besides waging war!" said Gregor.

"As in?" said Luxa.

"I don't have any off the top of my head," said Gregor. "But I bet I can come up with something a little less extreme."

"Well, when you do, I would love to hear it," said Luxa. "I am sure it will dazzle us all." She was mocking him. He might as well have been talking to Ripred.

Gregor stared at her a moment. "It was pretty easy, starting a war," he said.

"It was not difficult," said Luxa.

"I wonder what it will take to get out of it?" said Gregor.

"I doubt you will ever find out. Since you are going home," said Luxa. "We, on the other hand, must stay and live here."

They did not take a watch together that night. Gregor didn't want to argue with Luxa. What he wanted was to think up an answer to her question that *would* dazzle everyone. The problem was ... he didn't know what else could be done about the rats abusing the nibblers. If they didn't use force, how could the humans stop them? He knew the rats would not listen to talk. Since the plague, the humans had given the rats a lot of food and medicine to make up for unleashing the disease, but it had not erased the bitterness.

It was even more complicated because the rats did not have a leader to negotiate with. After King Gorger had died, the rats had splintered into groups. The plague had thrown them into even greater chaos. Now there was the Bane. He might be the next king. But then, what about rats that didn't follow him? Like Ripred and his gang. What about rats like Lapblood, who had been with Gregor on the quest to find the cure to the plague? She'd been trying to keep her pups alive. That's the main thing he knew about her. Would she support the Bane? If he was alive? If Ripred hadn't killed him?

Who exactly was Luxa declaring war on? The rats who had driven the nibblers off the cliff? Anyone who supported the Bane? Or just every rat, regardless of what they thought or stood for? Whatever Luxa had in mind, Gregor guessed that if a war really did begin, no one was going to take the time to interview a rat on its political position before they killed it.

Gregor found himself wishing very badly that he could talk to Hazard's father, Hamnet. Of course, Hamnet was gone. Killed months ago by the ants in a battle back in the jungle. Ten years earlier Hamnet had been one of Regalia's top soldiers. During a battle, he had inadvertently caused a dam to break, which resulted in the drowning deaths of not only an army of rats but also humans, bats, and the innocent rat pups sheltering in nearby caves. Hamnet had gone temporarily mad and then disappeared. Many years later, he had resurfaced in the jungle with his little son, Hazard, to act as Gregor's guide. Gregor remembered Vikus, who was Hamnet's father, begging him to return to Regalia. "What do you do here that you could not do there?" To which Hamnet had replied, "I do no harm. I do no more harm." Hamnet knew if he returned to Regalia, they would make him fight again.

Hamnet had tried to explain his position on war to Luxa. How it did no good. How innocent creatures died and, in the end, how it only increased the already intense hatred between the rats and the humans. Hamnet believed that the least amount of violence used, the better.

The things he'd talked about had made real sense to Gregor. Then an army of ants had appeared to destroy their precious plague cure and they had all ended up fighting, anyway. And that's when Hamnet had died. But what he had said . . . everything he had said . . . had been right. Deep inside, Gregor was sure of this. Only he did not know how to work his ideas into some kind of argument with Luxa. Not here. Not with the dead mice and the Bane running loose and everything. And why would she listen to him, anyway? Why would she listen to him say violence was a bad choice when he had hacked up a couple hundred snakes with a smile on his face? He drifted off to sleep feeling heartsick and confused. And without one dazzling idea.

When he awoke the next morning, the bats had already been fishing. Photos Glow-Glow and Zap were making loud smacking noises as they wolfed down their breakfast. Along with the fish, Howard had given them some other picnic treats that had spoiled . . . mushrooms in cream sauce, rotted greens.

The bats and Temp were only eating from the river now, but the remaining picnic food was running low. There were a few loaves of stale bread, some cheese, some dried vegetables, and a couple of cakes. Gregor looked over the supplies and thought about Boots wailing for food and water in the jungle. It had been unbearable. He sighed and picked up a raw fish, hacking off a piece with his sword. Better to save the picnic food for the kids.

Howard must have made a similar decision, because he was cracking open shellfish with a rock. "Try this," he said to Gregor, handing him a slimy thing on a half shell. "It is considered a delicacy at the Fount."

Gregor dumped the contents of the shell into his mouth. His teeth chased the slippery glob around his mouth for a few chews then he swallowed. Ugh. "I can see why," he said, trying to be polite.

"There are plenty," said Howard, shoving a stack toward Gregor.

"He does not want them, Howard; they are disgusting," said Luxa. She was expertly flaying the skin off a fish.

Gregor agreed with Luxa, but because he was angry with her and liked Howard he ate a few more of the shellfish just to prove her wrong. He drank some water to wash the taste out of his mouth, but then he could feel the things sloshing around in his stomach.

Cartesian awoke and seemed to have gained a little of his strength back. He was woozy from the medicine. "Where are the others?" he kept asking.

"We are going to get them now," said Luxa gently.

But he kept repeating, "Where? Where are the others?"

Howard got Cartesian to eat some ground-up fish

and gave him another dose of painkiller. Soon the mouse was sleeping again. "I'm afraid I shall have to sedate him on the entire journey back to Regalia," said Howard.

Space on the bats was becoming an issue. Hazard was still supposed to be lying down, so he and Luxa filled up Aurora's back. Gregor had Boots and Temp with him on Ares. And Howard settled Cartesian on Nike's back. "We are becoming a flying hospital ward," said Howard, "what with Hazard and Cartesian. We are lucky no one else is hurt."

Boots indignantly held up her finger. The nick was all but invisible now. "Me!" she said, shocked that she'd been overlooked.

"Oh, my goodness. Did I forget you, Boots? We had better put some medicine on that," said Howard.

It did not take more than an hour to cover the stretch of Hades Hall that was flat. Then the tunnel began to tilt upward as rapidly as it had dipped. If the trip down had required patient navigation from the bats, they had been allowed to coast for much of it. Now that they were flying upward, it required real physical exertion, but they seemed to be moving faster.

Thalia began to fall behind as the morning wore on. By lunch it was clear the little bat was done in.

"I know it is tight, but we are going to have to double up," said Howard, handing Gregor a nice, freshly cracked shellfish.

Gregor tossed it back without chewing. That was better somehow. "How do you want to do it?"

"We must put Thalia on Ares. Temp, could you ride on top of Thalia?" asked Howard.

Gregor remembered the first time Temp had flown. How much he had hated it. "Do it, I can, do it," said the cockroach, but Gregor knew it would be a challenge for the bug to be the top of a flying-bat pyramid.

"Cartesian is heavy, and I as well, so I do not think Nike can manage more than Boots," said Howard.

Gregor knew where that left him. With Luxa.

"If that is all right," said Howard.

"Fine," said Gregor.

Luxa was probably no more thrilled about the travel arrangements than Gregor, but there was nothing either of them could say. When it was time to move on, Gregor took a seat on Aurora's neck, facing forward. Luxa sat with her back to Gregor's, so she could amuse Hazard as they flew. The boy lay facing Luxa, with his feet on her lap.

For the first few hours, Luxa basically ignored Gregor. She passed the time by playing word games with Hazard. When that grew old, she told him the Underland equivalent of the famous fairy tale "Little Red Riding Hood." In Luxa's version, Little Red Riding Hood was a girl who left Regalia on her bat to visit her grandmother at the Fount. Against instructions, she strayed from the path. Instead of going into a forest, she was lured into tunnels by some lovely mushrooms. There she ran into the Big, Bad Rat. The rat didn't kill her because she was flying too high. Instead, he was so friendly that Little Red Riding Hood told him all about her plans. When Little Red Riding Hood arrived at her grandmother's house, the Big, Bad Rat was waiting for her, disguised as her grandmother. They did the whole "But, Grandmother, what big eyes you have!" routine. Then the grandmother appeared and killed the Big, Bad Rat and she and Little Red Riding Hood threw the rat's body in the river. The moral of the story — never trust a rat.

"But what about the good rats, Luxa?" asked Hazard. "Like Lapblood. She saved Boots's life in the jungle. Or Ripred. My father said he was a good rat and he is Vikus's friend," said Hazard.

"Yeah, what about them, Your Highness?" said Gregor. This was exactly one of the things that had been worrying him the night before.

"You must be very careful with rats, Hazard," said Luxa. "It would take many years and many acts of loyalty for me to consider a rat my friend. They teach their pups to despise us."

"You do the same thing," said Gregor. "Or are we supposed to feel sorry for the Big, Bad Rat?"

"You really have no idea how much they hate you, do you, Overlander?" said Luxa.

That gave him pause. "I know most of them do," Gregor admitted. "But there are a few I would call my friends."

"I wonder, would they call you their friend?" said Luxa.

Gregor let the question hang there. If you came down to it, it was hard to imagine Ripred or Lapblood actually calling him their friend. The only rat who might do that was Twitchtip, but she had been driven into the Dead Land by her own kind because of her extraordinary ability to smell and then she'd hooked up with humans on a mission to kill the Bane. She was not really a representative rat.

Hazard began to yawn and they stayed quiet while he went to sleep. It was not until the boy began to snore gently that Luxa spoke.

"You are very angry at me about declaring war," she said.

"I think it was the wrong thing to do," said Gregor.

"It has to happen, Gregor. Everyone knows it. The humans and gnawers cannot live in peace. One of us has to leave," said Luxa.

"Ripred said there was peace sometimes, in the past," said Gregor.

"But only for short periods. It never lasts," said Luxa. "We may as well get it over with. Have the war that will answer the question of who stays and who goes."

"Goes where, Luxa? If the humans lose, are you coming back up to the surface of the earth?" asked Gregor.

"I do not know. More likely, we would be forced into the Uncharted Lands, those beyond the edges of our maps. Perhaps, after some trial, another home could be found," said Luxa sadly.

"And if the rats lose, the ones who survive have to go into the Uncharted Lands?" said Gregor.

"I might keep Ripred around. As a pet," said Luxa.

Gregor had to smile. "A pet, huh?"

"Of course. I'd put bows on his tail and feed him shrimp in cream sauce and let him sleep by my pillow," said Luxa.

"He'd love that," said Gregor. He was laughing now. Something about the image of Ripred with bows on his tail.

"I had a pet lamb once and it was quite agreeable," said Luxa.

"Maybe you can teach him tricks," said Gregor.

"Maybe," giggled Luxa. "How to fetch and come when I whistle. My lamb could even jump through a hoop."

"It may take some time, but I'll bet he could learn that," said Gregor.

"Oh, yes, Ripred is very keen," said Luxa. She leaned against Gregor's backpack. He could feel her shaking as she laughed. After a while, she relaxed, but she didn't move away. She rested her head on the top of his shoulder, and he could feel her hair against his ear. It was nice. He sat very still, not wanting her to move away. Not wanting to think about wars. Or going home. Just wanting to sit close to her, in peace and quiet.

They flew a long while like that. The air grew warmer and a bad smell reached his nose. Like rotten eggs . . . that must be sulfur . . . and smoke. "We must be near the top of Hades Hall," Gregor thought. "Howard said the air would get foul as we came to the Firelands."

Aurora banked for a curve in the tunnel and at that moment the fireflies blacked out. Gregor could still see some, though. For a moment he was confused and thought they might be in the jungle. As his eyes adjusted to the dim reddish light, he realized they had left Hades Hall and entered a whole new world. It was like flying over some far-off planet. It was impossible to tell how long the cavern was, but it was only about twenty feet high. The ground was desolate, pitted with craters, covered with an ashy dust that swirled up in small clouds and then settled down again. It did not seem that anything could survive here.

But something was very much alive. Gregor could

just make out the creatures' backs a few hundred yards away. They were rodents of some kind. A number of small ones were gathering around a gray figure, which towered over them. At first Gregor thought they had caught up to the mice and one of their rat guards. Then the gray figure gave a shake, freeing itself of a layer of ashes and revealing a pearl-white coat.

16

Aurora made a sharp turn and they landed in a hollow space in the wall to their right. It was barely deep enough to be called a cave, but it did shelter them from the rats' direct line of vision. Ares and Nike were quick to join them.

"The dust should prevent them from smelling us," said Howard.

Gregor could hear the crowd of rats he had seen talking. But there were no angry cries to attack.

"And they must not have seen us," Gregor whispered.

"No," replied Aurora. "Their eyes are fixed upon . . . upon . . . is it him?"

"Yeah, that's the Bane," said Gregor, sliding off

her back. Howard and Luxa joined him as he peered around the stone opening to get a better look.

"Let me see!" said Boots, lighting up her scepter.

"No, Boots! We need it to stay dark." Gregor quickly confiscated the scepter and slipped it into his backpack. "I'll give it back soon," he promised.

"He is enormous," said Howard.

"He's even bigger than the last time I saw him," said Gregor.

"What? When he was a pup?" asked Luxa.

Of course, they didn't know about his meeting the Bane beneath Regalia. He hadn't told anyone. "I'll tell you later," he muttered.

Luxa scowled. "Maybe you should tell us now. Have you seen him — ?"

But Howard cut her off. "Hush, he means to speak."

The Bane had leaped up onto a shelf of rock before the other rats. "Gnawers! Gnawers!" called the Bane. "I beg a moment of your time!" His voice had matured since that day Gregor had watched him fight with Ripred. It was low and deep and commanded attention. At its sound, more rats appeared out of the wasteland and joined those already assembled, swelling their ranks to several hundred.

"A moment of your time, to give you my thanks," said the Bane. "For being here. For standing beside me. Because what am I, what are any of us, if we stand alone?"

The rats had settled down now and were giving the Bane their full attention. The white rat lowered himself onto all fours and began to pace back and forth before the crowd. His manner was almost casual, his tone philosophical. "I know what we once were. The unquestioned rulers of the Underland. And I know what we have been of late. Weak. Hungry. Diseased. At the mercy of our enemies. Tortured by humans, and mocked by creatures who in the past would not have dared to look us in the eye."

A murmur ran through the crowd.

"We've never been liked," continued the Bane. "But we were always feared. Until Gorger died. When the others stopped fearing us, they stopped respecting us as well. Does it bother you when the crawlers laugh as they strip our rivers clean of fish?"

A few of the rats called out, "Yes!"

"When the cutters claim land we have held for centuries?" asked the Bane.

"Yes!" More rats were joining in.

"When the humans infect us with a germ that ravages our species and then try to smooth things over with a few baskets of grain?" said the Bane, his voice rising in anger.

"Yes!" Most of the crowd had answered. Gregor could see the rats' agitation, their restless bodies, their swinging tails.

"How many of you lost pups?" asked the Bane. "And how many of you still call yourself parents? Which is worse? To watch them suffer and die quickly or to see them die slowly, stripped of pride, groveling at the feet of inferior creatures? Is that the life we want for our children?"

Several rats shouted, "No!" while others called for the death of the humans.

"The humans. The humans," said the Bane in disgust. "We knew from the moment they arrived that the Underland was not big enough to hold us both. And we will deal with the humans in the proper time. But there are others who must be taken care of first. . . ." He stopped pacing and planted himself directly before the crowd. "If we ask ourselves who caused our troubles, we must ask ourselves who benefited by our suffering. Who found fertile lands to feed in? Whose numbers increased while ours diminished? Whose pups thrived while our own died of starvation and disease? You know who I'm talking about!"

Cries of "The nibblers!" came from the crowd.

"Yes, the nibblers! My father used to joke that the only good nibbler he ever saw was a dead nibbler," said the Bane wryly.

Ugly laughter rippled across the crowd.

"But maybe if he had used his time acting instead of joking, we would not be here today!" continued the Bane. "Tell me, if you can, why not one nibbler pup died of the plague? Why, when gnawers and fliers and even humans writhed in agony, they alone remained well? I'll tell you why. Because it was their plague. Everyone blames the humans; the fools even blame themselves. But where did that germ come from? It had to come from somewhere. The humans did not create it in their laboratories. We all know where the plague is born. In the jungle. And who, until quite

213

recently, made the jungle their home? The nibblers. They found that germ. They gave it to the humans to turn into a weapon to be used against us. But not before they had the cure — all along they had the cure — all along they were safe and smug while they watched us die!"

There was a confused rumbling in the crowd. Gregor had the feeling that this was the first time this theory had been presented to the rats.

"Why should that surprise us?" said the Bane disdainfully. "Haven't they always plotted against us? Didn't they ally themselves with the humans the moment Sandwich arrived and offer to become his spies? Aren't they, even to this day, the eyes and ears of Regalia? Of all the creatures who take pleasure in our humiliation, I can stand the nibblers the least!"

This was greeted with a roar of agreement. The Bane lifted his voice above the din. "We have tried to drive them from our lands again and again, but it is never far enough. I say, this time we drive them to a place that allows no return!"

The rats were being whipped into a frenzy.

"Do some of you hesitate? Do some of you think another solution can be found? Remember that we have looked for gentler alternatives in the past, and think where that got us!" said the Bane.

The Bane reared up on his hind legs to his full height. "It is the law of nature. The strong determine the fate of the weak. Are we the weak? Are we the weak?"

The rats were leaping into the air and screaming back, "No! No!"

"Then gather the strength within you and fight with me! We have many enemies. The battle ahead of us is long and bloody. It will be difficult. But when you start to falter, find the hatred inside of you and draw power from it. Think of how the crawlers laugh, the humans smirk, the nibblers grow fat while we starve, and see then if you do not have the stomach for what lies ahead!"

The crowd began to scream for the Bane.

"You say you want me to lead you? I will lead you! But a leader is only as strong as the force that stands behind him. Are you strong?" bellowed the Bane.

"Yes!"

"Do you stand behind me?" he shouted.

"Yes!"

"Then let our enemies do what they will. No creature in the Underland can stop us!" The Bane tilted back his head and gave a bloodcurdling battle cry as the rats went wild below him.

Gregor slumped back against the wall inside the cave, breathless and dazed. "Oh, no." It was not just the viciousness of the Bane's speech that stunned Gregor; it was its persuasiveness. "Twirltongue has been coaching him," Gregor thought. "Putting ideas in his head. Teaching him how to say them. And now he believes it all."

Luxa's and Howard's faces were shocked and pale. "He is a monster," said Howard. "Did you hear his words? Is he insane? How can he blame the plague on the nibblers?"

"The others believed him," said Luxa.

"I half-believed him myself," said Ares. "He made it seem so logical."

"What will he do to the nibblers?" said Aurora. "What does he mean, to drive them to a place that allows no return?"

"I do not know. Out of the Underland for certain," said Howard.

"And into the Uncharted Lands," said Luxa.

The rat noise began to die down a little.

Boots tugged on Howard's sleeve. "I'm hungry."

He quickly pressed his finger against her lips. "Shh. We must not be discovered, Boots. Like Hide and Go Seek, you understand?"

Boots grinned excitedly and gave a little bounce. "Shh!" she said.

"Shh!" repeated Howard.

But there was someone it was not so easy to quiet. Cartesian had been stirring in his drug-induced sleep. The Bane's words must have filtered into his dreams. "No!" he cried out. "No!"

"Wake him, Howard! They will hear!" said Luxa.

Howard shook Cartesian and the mouse bolted up in terror. "Where are the others?" he screamed, his head turning from side to side. "Where are the others!"

"No, Cartesian, hush. They are safe. You are safe," whispered Howard urgently.

But the mouse was not reachable. "Where are the others!" he insisted.

Gregor allowed just one eye to slip around the cave wall. It was enough to see that the army of rats was galloping for them. "They heard! Mount up! Get out of here!"

They reloaded the bats in a moment. Gregor grabbed Boots because it was all Howard could do to keep the frantic Cartesian on Nike's back. "Where are the others! Where are the others!"

The bats shot out over the cavern but had no idea where to go. As soon as they were airborne, they were recognized. The rats began to shout, "The Warrior! Queen Luxa!" Some were laughing, almost crazed by their good fortune of trapping such excellent quarry so easily.

"Where to?" called Ares, circling the air with Thalia and Temp clinging to his back.

Gregor saw what looked like some tunnel openings along the walls, but the rats had stirred up the ashes from the ground into a cloud, making it even harder to see. "We need more light!" he said, expecting the bright shiner beams to turn on. But there was no response. "Shiners!" He turned his head from side to side, trying to locate the bugs. "Where are they?"

"Gone!" said Howard in disgust. "They headed back into Hades Hall the moment we left the cave!"

"Stupid bugs!" said Gregor. But what had he expected? This was not the kind of situation Photos Glow-Glow or Zap would hang around for. He snapped on the flashlight at his belt and shone it around the cavern.

Below them, hundreds of seething rats called out curses and leaped as high as they were able. Others had split off from the main group and were running to block the mouths of the tunnels along the walls. A few were already impassable.

"Should we go back to Hades Hall?" shouted Gregor.

"No, we will be trapped there for sure!" said Luxa.

"Then pick a tunnel, Luxa!" said Howard. He was literally pinning Cartesian to Nike's back now. "Make haste!"

"The one on your left, Aurora! Take it!" Luxa ordered.

The rats had not quite reached the tunnel entrance as the bats swept into it. But they were only seconds away and there would be no turning back. Gregor could hear them calling from the entrance, laughing and taunting. It gave him a bad feeling.

"They don't seem too unhappy about our escape," he said.

"That can only mean one thing," said Luxa. "Whatever lies in this tunnel wants us as dead as the rats do."

The words had just left her mouth when Ares

gave a warning. "Arm yourselves! Stingers! Arm yourselves!"

The bats swooped into a huge chamber. Waiting on the floor with their tails poised in the air were a pair of giant scorpions.

CHAPTER

17

The two scorpions were about ten and twelve feet long. In addition to eight legs, each had a pair of pinchers snapping before it. But Gregor knew their most deadly weapons were their tails, which began to swing the moment the bats entered the chamber. He caught a glimpse of a foot-long stinger projecting from the end of a tail as it whizzed by him. Most of the scorpions in the Overland just gave you a terrible sting, but some had poison toxic enough to kill a human. And they were tiny beside these creatures. Whatever kind of venom these scorpions were packing, Gregor was sure one shot would be enough to finish off any of his party.

He could tell the bats thought so, too, because they were expending all their energy dodging those tails, even if it meant taking a dive down into pincher range.

Gregor had his right arm wrapped around Boots and was holding the flashlight in his left hand. He struggled to pull his sword off his left hip without letting go of her, but she was leaning curiously over the side of Nike's neck.

"Who's that?" she said. "Spiders?"

"Sit up, Boots!" he said.

"We need more light!" said Luxa.

"In my backpack!" said Gregor as he finally worked his sword free. Only now he had to hold his wiggly little sister with his flashlight arm. "Can you sit still!"

"Are they spiders, Gre-go?" Boots asked. "Like 'Itsy-Bitsy Spider'?"

"No!" said Gregor. "Boots, turn around! Hang on to me like a monkey!" She obeyed, but she still kept craning her neck around to see the "spiders."

He could feel Luxa digging in his pack and a few seconds later another beam of light brightened the cave. "Geez," he said as he got a clear look at the larger of the two scorpions. He was even more formidable when you could see him better. His body was covered in an armor shell, and he had about five pairs of eyes. That multiple-eye thing always freaked Gregor out.

"Hold on, Boots! I'm going to let go!" he said. This caught her attention. Maybe she remembered the flood and what had happened the last time he'd let go of her, because she locked her arms and legs around him so tightly he could hardly breathe. "Good," he squeaked out.

"Sever their tails!" he heard Howard shout.

"Right!" Gregor said, but he could not get himself into attack mode. What with Aurora flipping right and left to avoid the stingers and Boots squeezing the air out of him . . . plus he had very limited motion with his sword arm since he had to fight around her. "I hope Luxa and Howard can take them," he thought. But he soon realized that was not going to happen. Howard had not even managed to draw his sword, because he was still trying to restrain Cartesian. Luxa was facing backward on Aurora, not the ideal fighting position, trying to keep herself and Hazard on board.

"Gregor, can you attack?" said Howard.

"I'm trying," said Gregor, chopping in the general direction of a tail. He missed by a mile. As to becoming a rager — the idea was laughable. He felt none of the intense focus and fear that sometimes brought on the condition. Instead, he felt trapped in a really silly horror movie.

"Baby spiders!" said Boots, as if making a pleasant discovery. "See the babies?"

"They're not babies," he said, and then had the awful thought that these were babies and she had spotted even larger scorpions, like the thirty-foot kind, headed their way.

"Hi, babies!" said Boots.

"Where? Where are the babies?" said Gregor.

"On the mama," said Boots, pointing. "See? Babies."

Gregor shone his light on the smaller scorpion's back and for the first time knew what Boots was talking about. About a dozen little scorpions were squirming around on the scorpion's shell. "Oh, great," he thought. The only thing worse than fighting a giant scorpion was fighting a giant scorpion who was trying to protect her young.

"I sing the babies to sleep," announced Boots.

"Fine, sing," said Gregor, thinking it would be better if she was occupied if he ever did make contact with one of those tails. Any sort of violence upset her. She wouldn't want him to hurt her "spiders."

It wasn't until Boots launched into her rendition of the "Itsy-Bitsy Spider" that Gregor realized what a bad idea it was. The song required hand motions as the spider climbed the waterspout, as the rain fell down. And to do them, Boots let go of his neck.

"Hang on, Boots! Hang on!" he cried. But it was too late. Just as the sun was coming up in the song, Aurora did a full body roll to the side to avoid a tail, and Boots fell off.

"Me!" said Boots as she flapped her arms, just as she had back in the arena.

"Boots!" cried Gregor.

Ares dove to catch Boots and managed to scoop the little girl up on his head, but the motion so startled Thalia that she fell off his back, taking Temp with her. Neither Aurora nor Nike had any means of catching the pair, so the little bat and the cockroach landed with a thud on the stone floor.

"Thalia!" screamed Hazard. "Fly!"

"Hold on, Temp!" said Gregor.

Thalia scurried to her feet, and Temp scuttled sideways a couple of yards, unsure of where to go. Ares veered back, claws extended to rescue them, but it was too late. Lightning fast, the mother scorpion attacked and pinned Thalia's wings to the ground with her pinchers. Her tail flipped over her head, poised for the kill. Thalia let out a piteous cry, knowing she was moments from death.

"No!" shrieked Hazard. "No!" He wrenched himself free of Luxa and leaped off Aurora's back. Fortunately, Aurora was only about twelve feet above the ground and he managed to land on his hands and feet. He scrambled straight over to Thalia, kneeled above her head, and extended his hands up to block the stinger. "No!"

Luxa had flipped after Hazard seconds after she'd lost her hold on him. She landed solidly on her feet and made for the scorpion, her sword ready to attack. The scorpion let out an angry hiss and Hazard suddenly turned and grabbed Luxa's sword arm. "Don't! Don't attack her!" he said frantically. "No one attack!" Still clinging to Luxa's arm, he turned his head back to the scorpion and began to make a bizarre series of hissing sounds.

The scorpion's tail quivered in place for a moment, as if in indecision. "Put your swords away! All of you!" said Hazard. Luxa hesitated. "Please, Luxa!" She reluctantly returned the sword to her belt, her hand still clenched on the hilt.

Hazard let out another round of hisses. The scorpion slowly let her tail relax behind her, although she did not release Thalia.

By this time Gregor and Aurora had landed. The first thing Gregor did as he slid off Aurora's back was sheathe his sword.

"Can you talk to her, Hazard?" Gregor asked.

"I don't know. I'm speaking Hisser, like I did with Frill. But I don't think the words are exactly the same for stingers," said Hazard.

A thought struck Gregor. Boots was right about one thing: Scorpions had eight legs like spiders. . . . They were different species, but maybe . . . "Try talking in Spider."

Hazard began to drum on his chest and issued a series of vibrating sounds. The scorpion shifted slightly from side to side, seeming genuinely confused.

"Temp! Temp! Try Crawler speech on it," said Howard.

Temp pattered up to join Hazard, clicking tentatively. Hazard joined in; he was almost fluent in

Cockroach now. And of course, someone else would not be left out.

"Me, too! Me, too!" said Boots. She jumped off of Ares's head, and Gregor just barely caught her.

"Hey!" he said. "You can't just jump off —"

But she was already out of his arms, running over to the mother scorpion. "Let me talk! Let me talk!" Boots squealed, hopping eagerly from foot to foot. A stream of clicking intermingled with English poured out of her mouth. It was so frenetic, Hazard and Temp left off and let her go. Boots rattled on for about a minute, gesturing to the babies and singing little bits of "Itsy-Bitsy Spider" and click, click, clicking away, and then suddenly she stopped, her hands clasped together, her chin forward, as if she was eagerly expecting an answer.

There was a long pause, and then one of the scorpions behind Gregor made a few clicks. Then everybody started babbling or clicking or hissing until Howard called for silence.

Nike came in for a landing. Cartesian had worked himself into a state of exhaustion and lay limp on her back, glazed eyes staring into space. Howard slid off the bat and took Hazard's hand.

"What is it, Hazard? What do they understand?" said Howard.

"I think that they both understand some Hisser, I can't tell about the Spinner talk, and the big one there knows Crawler," said Hazard.

"All right, then," said Howard. "Ask them to free Thalia. Tell them we mean no harm and only wish to pass."

Hazard communicated this to the scorpion who had clicked. They did not hear him respond. But he must have said something to the mother scorpion, because she released her grip on Thalia. The little bat fluttered right into Aurora's wings and buried her head.

The scorpion began to click again.

"He wants to know how we came here," said Hazard.

"Tell him," said Luxa. "Tell him the rats chased us here, sure that the stingers would kill us."

Hazard transmitted the message and the scorpion replied after a minute. "The gnawers are their enemies, too. They have recently forced the stingers out of some of their lands."

"Have they seen the nibblers?" asked Luxa.

Hazard talked a moment with the scorpion and

said, "They have. The rats drove them by here only yesterday. And it does not go well with the nibblers. Many are sick or injured."

Boots, who had been very patient for a three-year-old, could no longer contain herself. She went off again, clicking and singing and pointing at the mother scorpion.

"What is your problem?" said Gregor, scooping her up.

"She wants to pet the babies," said Hazard.

"What? They're scorpions, Boots. You don't pet them!" said Gregor. But he was wrong again. A few minutes later, after some negotiation and assurances that they were too little to sting, Boots was sitting on the mother scorpion's back cooing to the babies as she patted their shells. Gregor guessed he shouldn't be surprised when he remembered how readily she'd taken to the cockroaches. And they were full-grown.

Hazard came over to join her and seemed to be able to talk to the mother some by hissing. Howard and Temp continued to exchange information with the bilingual scorpion. Luxa got out the last, very stale cake and laid it out as a peace offering for the scorpions. All thoughts of fighting were gone.

Luxa licked a bit of frosting from her finger and shook her head. "It reminds me of what Hamnet told us in the jungle," she said to Gregor.

"What's that?" he said.

"About how many creatures do not wish to fight," said Luxa.

"But you'll never know if you show up waving your sword around," said Gregor, remembering. "I guess it's a good thing we were all so useless."

"Yes, if we could have actually fought, no doubt someone would now be dead," said Luxa.

"The stingers have agreed to let us stay here and rest before we move on," said Howard.

Ares and Nike got directions to a stream that ran through a nearby tunnel and soon returned with fish. They had a sort of picnic with the scorpions: raw fish and cake, and cold water to drink.

Boots would not eat the fish herself but loved feeding it to the baby scorpions. They took the fish but couldn't really swallow it. The scorpions seemed to need to drink their food like the spiders had. Injecting it with some liquid until it turned to goo. So the babies stole bites from the pile of gunk in front of their mother. Gregor just tried not to look at it.

Hazard and Temp continued to act as interpreters.

"We know so little of stingers," said Howard. "Ask them, do they always live here or are they wanderers?"

"They say they have always lived here. Usually it is very peaceful. No one bothers them. But of late, the whole Underland comes to their doorstep. Shiners, nibblers, gnawers, crawlers, fliers, and even killers," said Hazard. He bit into a raw fish as if he'd said nothing out of the ordinary. But Gregor could see the look of shock on Howard's and Luxa's faces.

"Killers," said Gregor. "Who are they? Is there some other monster running around out here?"

"Oh, no, Gregor," said Hazard simply. "It's us. We humans are the killers."

18

"What do you mean, we're the killers?" asked Gregor.

"You know how things have two names. Rats are gnawers. Bats are fliers. Most people call Temp a crawler, but my mother called him a cockroach like you do," said Hazard. "And she said 'spider' like Boots."

"When Sandwich came down, he used 'spider' as well," said Howard. "But in time, 'spinner' became the more popular term."

"In the Underland, creatures are named for what they do," said Hazard. "That's why they're the stingers," said Hazard, nodding to a scorpion. "And Ares is a flier. And we're killers."

"I've never heard that before," said Gregor.

"We do not like the name, so our friends do not

call us by it. And our enemies do not use it to our faces, either, because it makes the humans seem too strong," said Howard.

"Killers, huh?" Gregor said to Luxa. He had seen too much in the Underland to give the humans some sort of "good guy" status. They were capable of doing plenty of damage. But what had they done to have earned the name "killers"? Had they really killed more than any of the other creatures?

"It is a very old name. As Howard says, we do not like it," she said. "I am surprised to hear you use it, Hazard."

"My father used it sometimes," said Hazard.

"Well, your father was not . . . he was not really one of us anymore," said Luxa. "I mean, he did not want to live with us."

"No. He did not like being a killer," said Hazard.

"Stop it! Stop saying that!" said Luxa.

Hazard looked at her in surprise. She almost never rebuked him. "Why? It is true. Humans are known for their killing."

"It is a very old name, Hazard," said Howard. "One we would like to see fade away entirely."

"I don't know how that will happen," said Hazard

earnestly. "It's what most creatures call you in their own tongues, even if they do not use it in English. The hissers, the spinners, the crawlers, almost everyone."

"Well, that is an interesting piece of news," said Luxa, shooting a look at Temp.

"An old word, it be, old," said Temp uncomfortably.

"How could you not know that?" asked Hazard.

"Because you and your dad were the first humans who ever learned to speak another creature's language," said Gregor. "Better let it drop now, Hazard."

"I'm sorry," Hazard said, squeezing Luxa's hand.

"It is of no account," she said, giving him a hug. But Gregor could tell she was still unhappy about the whole conversation.

It was not exactly lifting Gregor's spirits, either. If the humans were known as killers, then what did that make him? Their warrior? Their rager? A killer among killers? For the first time he began to wonder what this war Luxa had declared would personally mean for him. Was it assumed that, as the warrior, he would participate? He had never fought in a major war. He'd only been in a couple battles and never faced off with an army of rats. He was, in reality, very inexperienced, but he doubted that would matter. What did the Underlanders expect of him? Did he have a special role? Like possibly . . . killing the Bane? Gregor pushed the idea from his brain. No point thinking about that until he was back in Regalia with Vikus to talk him through "The Prophecy of Time." And then what? Then he would have to decide whether he was in or out.

It had been a long day. Starting with that breakfast of slimy shellfish, then the flight up Hades Hall, the Bane's speech, the rat attack, and the scorpions. Somewhere in that mess was the lovely peaceful time he had shared with Luxa, when they'd leaned back-to-back in silence. He wanted to pull the experience out and examine it and relive it. But the minute he'd curled up beside Boots, he fell fast asleep.

In the morning, the scorpions helped them work out their next move. The rats would have the mouth of the tunnel blocked, just in case any of them survived. But the scorpions knew the area far better than the rats. The best idea seemed to be to follow a series of tunnels deeper into the Firelands. Although it would mean a longer flight back to Regalia, they should have larger open spaces to fly in and less of a chance of being trapped by the rats. Luxa did not bring up her plan to pursue the mice, but Gregor knew she still meant to find them.

"And they say be watchful of the currents," said Hazard.

No one was too worried about the currents, though. Gregor had ridden the airstreams up and down to the Underland dozens of times now. He actually kind of liked the currents.

As they were saying their good-byes, Luxa had Hazard translate a message for them. "Tell them from this day on, the humans consider the stingers their allies. Tell them we wish for nothing but peaceful relations between us. Tell them when they let Thalia live, they entered our hearts."

Hazard relayed the message. The scorpions came back with a similar, if less emotional, pledge. But then, since they'd had very little experience with the scorpions and there were several different languages to take into account, no one could really judge its tone. You had a scorpion speaking in Crawler to a seven-year-old boy who had only recently learned Crawler and spoke a mixture of Overland and Underland English. Things could have been lost in translation.

Gregor just considered it a huge victory that everyone

got out of the situation alive. And there did seem to be the beginning of trust. Boots's affection for the babies had made a good impression. The scorpions were trying to help them evade the rats.

"You know who'd have loved that? Your grandpa," Gregor told Luxa as they started down a tunnel on Aurora's back.

"Yes, Vikus is very fond of peaceful resolutions. So am I. I just believe that in his eagerness to achieve them, my grandfather can trust too soon. Remember when we visited the spinners? We ended up as their prisoners," said Luxa.

"But they didn't kill us," said Gregor.

"They almost killed me!" said Luxa.

"Well, you were trying to escape," said Gregor.

"And then it took Gorger and his army slaughtering the spinners for them to ally themselves with us," said Luxa.

"They might not have ever done that, though, if they didn't trust Vikus," said Gregor.

"Perhaps not," said Luxa.

"I'm just saying, it's nice when nobody gets killed," said Gregor.

"That is pretty talk for a warrior," said Luxa. "Not

the sort of thing you will want to be shouting out before a battle." She mimicked his accent. " 'Remember, it's nice when nobody gets killed!' "

Gregor laughed. "Who knows? Maybe that's exactly what I should be shouting before a battle."

He was in a strangely good mood given the circumstances. He was far from home, surrounded by enemies, many of his companions were wounded, his family was worried sick, the mice were being driven who knew where, the Bane had turned into some sort of evil genius leader, and there was some ominous prophecy lying in wait for him. And here he was joking around with Luxa. Maybe it was just the relief of still being alive. Or maybe it was something else. . . .

Luxa was leaning against his backpack again, her head on his shoulder. Howard flew by and gave Gregor a disapproving look. What? He hadn't made the seating arrangements. Howard had. It was more comfortable riding with someone to lean on. Probably Gregor was in for another speech about dates and queens and things. About how nothing was right about him liking Luxa.

"Oh, who cares? My mom will probably send me home the second we reach Regalia, anyway," thought Gregor. But the idea didn't make him feel happy.

The walls and floor of the tunnel began to transform from a dull gray to a shiny black. Light from Gregor's flashlight and Boots's scepter danced off the surfaces and reflected to other spots. When they landed at a spring-fed pool for a break, Gregor stooped down and ran his fingers over the surface beneath his feet. It was smooth. Almost slick.

Luxa examined the ground beside him. "It is like black glass."

"I think it might be obsidian," said Gregor.

Boots quickly discovered the slipperiness of the floor. "Look, Gre-go, I ice-skate!" she said, sliding wildly over the black surface, waving her scepter.

"I want to try, too!" said Hazard.

Howard grabbed Hazard before he could work up much speed. "Oh, no, you do not, Hazard. The last thing you need is another head injury."

Luxa was still focused on the floor. "What is obsidian?" she asked Gregor.

"It's a kind of rock you only find around volcanoes. It's made from cooled lava," said Gregor.

"You must be right. The Firelands are known for their volcanoes," said Luxa.

"Active volcanoes?" asked Gregor. "Do they still work?"

"Why would they not?" asked Luxa. "They cannot break."

"They can become dormant. Asleep," said Gregor.

"I do not know, then. No human has ever stayed long enough to study them. The air is too bad for extended visits," said Luxa.

Suddenly all four of the bats lifted their chins, usually a sign they had sensed something alarming.

"What is it, Aurora?" asked Luxa.

"I do not know. Some creature moves within," said the bat, nodding in the direction Boots was heading.

"I cannot detect its shape," said Ares, in a puzzled tone.

"Come back, Boots!" called Gregor. But either she wasn't listening or she was ignoring him. "Hey, I'm not kidding!" he said, taking off after her. After about ten steps, he lost his footing and landed on his rear end. "Boots!"

"Wheee!" said Boots as she spun across the floor, and then suddenly she gave an "Uh-oh!" and dropped out of sight.

"Where is she?" exclaimed Hazard.

"Ow!" said the little voice from the dark. "We bumped." Her sandals pattered around. "I know you!" she said. "Oh, ow. . . ." But this second "ow" was a sound not of pain but of sympathy.

Gregor ran toward her voice and would have fallen as well had Howard not caught him by the arm and lifted him back. They were at the edge of a large pit that was about twenty feet deep. The obsidian walls were very steep and smooth.

"Gre-go! Gre-go!" Boots was trying to climb out of the pit, but she slid back down its side almost immediately. "Gre-go, see who is here! Ow!" She pressed her hand against her teeth and then pointed her scepter at the creature beside her.

A scrawny rat lay a few feet to her right, panting for air. His front teeth were way overgrown, at least by a foot, and had locked together, spreading his mouth in a horrible grimace and distorting his face painfully.

But Gregor could still make out the scar on the agonized face. "Ripred," he said.

The rat locked eyes with him but was unable to speak.

"Don't move," said Gregor. "We're coming."

PART 3
The Queen

CHAPTER

19

Gregor turned to Howard, figuring he was the best person to handle a medical crisis. "What do we do?"

But even Howard was at a loss. "I do not know. Perhaps we can file his teeth down some way. I doubt pulling them is an option, but if we must —"

"Oh, move aside!" said Luxa impatiently, pushing by them. She stepped sideways onto the slope and slid, one leg extended, one leg bent at the knee, straight down into the pit. She landed on her feet and drew her sword, sweeping it back as if to attack. "Stand back, Boots!" she ordered, and the little girl cleared out of the way. For a moment, Gregor thought Luxa was going to kill Ripred. She had certainly done nothing to stop the rat from suffocating in quicksand when they'd met up with her in the jungle that time. But instead of cutting Ripred's throat, her blade smashed into his locked teeth. The ones on the left half of his mouth cracked off in jagged points. Ripred emitted a guttural sound of pain at the impact but lifted his head up for her to swing again. Luxa's second hit shattered through the other half of Ripred's teeth, and he slumped forward on the ground, gasping. The uneven edges left by the blow cut into his gums, causing them to bleed, but his jaws were freed.

Ripred stared at Luxa for a minute, then spoke in a hoarse whisper. "You remember . . . in the jungle . . . you said you would be in my debt . . ."

"If you told me Hamnet's story. About the Garden of the Hesperides," said Luxa.

"Consider the debt . . . paid in full," said Ripred.

"A story for your life? That is not a fair exchange. I believe you owe me now," said Luxa.

"I hate that," sighed Ripred.

"I bet you do," said Luxa with a grin. "Ares, can you bring him up?"

Ares flew down, clamped his claws into Ripred's shoulders, and hauled him out of the pit while Aurora brought up Luxa and Boots.

"Water," was Ripred's first request.

Howard opened up a skin and held it while the rat drank his fill. "I have a rough stone, a small one, for sharpening blades. Shall I try to even up your teeth?"

Gregor knew it must be killing Ripred, who was so relentlessly powerful, so universally feared, to be sitting there while a human filed his teeth. Guessing an audience would only make things worse, Gregor mobilized the others. He asked the bats and Temp to fish in a nearby stream. Hazard and Boots helped Luxa fill the water bags. Cartesian was too medicated to really matter.

When the fish started to arrive, Gregor busied himself by chopping some up into tiny pieces. He stirred in some water and a handful of dry bread crumbs. By the time Howard had the edges of Ripred's teeth smoothed out, Gregor had a nice big bowl of fish mash waiting for him. Boots wanted to feed him, but Gregor thought that would be too much for the rat, so he scooped the food into Ripred's mouth himself. Although Gregor had made several pounds of fish mash, several more bowls were needed before Ripred was satisfied.

"All right. I'm all right now," he said, finally pushing away the bowl, with a few remaining bites of mash stuck to the bottom. The rat gingerly opened and closed his jaws. "Can I see that rock?" Howard gave him the rock, and Ripred worked a little on his teeth, shaping them into his usual style. After a while, he stopped gnawing and sized up the group for the first time. "So, what brings the Children's Crusade into the Firelands? I don't flatter myself you were looking for me."

"We got lost on a picnic," said Luxa.

"I know I'm down, but don't humiliate me further with transparent lies, Your Highness," said Ripred. "Don't I always tell you the truth?"

"You lied to me about 'The Prophecy of Blood.' You said I just had to come to a meeting when you knew I had to go to the jungle," said Gregor.

"Not exactly. If you think back, my comments were very open to interpretation. And you happen to be easily misled," said Ripred. "As for the queen, who is difficult to lead anywhere . . . I have always been and intend to be entirely straightforward."

Luxa considered this for a moment. "We went looking for the nibblers," she said. "One sent my crown, as a plea for help. The jungle nibblers have disappeared.

Those by the Fount are being driven here to the Firelands."

"My little charge, the Bane, doesn't fancy them much, does he?" said Ripred. "And what do you mean to do by following them?"

"Draw the Regalian armies after me," said Luxa. "I said 'The Vow to the Dead' in Hades Hall."

"Did you indeed?" said Ripred. "It seems like only yesterday you were a baby bouncing on your grandpa's knee. And now you're starting wars. They grow up so fast."

"And what would you have done?" Luxa asked.

"Now I'm in an awkward position, Your Highness. Ordinarily, I'd have said I'd have hunted down the Bane myself and killed him, hopefully disabling the serpent by beheading it. Of course, as you've just rescued me from a pit where I was being slowly tortured to death on the Bane's command . . . my advice seems to have less impact," said Ripred.

"You could not leap out?" asked Howard.

"No, the walls are too high to clear, too slick to climb. And there wasn't so much as a pebble for me to gnaw on. So my teeth kept growing. Mine locked, as opposed to growing up through my brain. Lucky for me, if not the Bane," said Ripred.

"He put you in there? He outfought you?" asked Gregor.

"Who, the Bane? Please. His soldiers did," said Ripred.

"But . . . no one can touch you!" said Gregor.

"Even a rager can be outnumbered, Gregor," said Ripred. "I start to crack at about four hundred to one. You, I hear, crumbled in the face of three. Of course, there were extenuating circumstances."

"What is he talking about?" asked Luxa.

Gregor didn't answer. It was too embarrassing to think that Ripred knew about his episode with Twirltongue. That all the rats knew and were laughing at him.

"You might as well tell her, before someone else does," said Ripred.

"Three rats kicked my butt in the tunnels under Regalia," said Gregor.

"What were you and three rats doing under Regalia?" asked Luxa accusingly.

"I'll take that. See, I'd brought the Bane with me to echolocation lessons, so Gregor could meet him and help me kill him. Unfortunately, my pearly friend sneaked off in the night. I had to chase him, of course, and when Gregor came down the next day for the assassination, he found not me or the Bane but three of the Bane's pals," said Ripred. "Now the warrior, as I understand it, was actually doing quite well, until . . . ?" He looked pointedly at Gregor.

"Until I lost my light," muttered Gregor.

"And at that moment he realized that all along he'd been wrong about being so uncooperative during his lessons and that . . . ?" Ripred waited again.

"You were right, Ripred," said Gregor.

"'You were right, Ripred,'" said the rat slowly, savoring every word. "You know, I think it's all been worth it just to hear those words, from that mouth," said Ripred. "Any more fish mash? I'm hungry again."

Ripred stuck his nose in the remaining fish mash and lapped it up.

Gregor could feel Luxa's eyes burning holes in him.

"So when did you plan on telling us about the Bane and his three friends running around under our palace?" said Luxa.

"Never, if possible," said Gregor. "It didn't seem to matter."

"It would matter a great deal to you, if it was your home," said Luxa.

"Vikus said the door was solid," said Gregor.

"And was that door barred when you were fighting those rats?" asked Luxa.

"No," admitted Gregor. If he had not waylaid them with the lamp, nothing would have stopped the rats from entering the palace. "But I didn't know they were there. I thought it would only be Ripred and the Bane."

"They are everywhere, Gregor," said Howard softly. And that's when Gregor knew how careless he had been. Howard didn't fly off the handle like Luxa. If he was concerned, there was a real problem.

"I always left the door unbarred during my lessons," said Gregor. "Vikus never told me different."

"Because he knew I was there and I wouldn't let anyone up to the palace. Lay off the warrior. Blame me, blame Vikus, if you want to blame someone," said Ripred.

"I blame you all," said Luxa.

"If you must. But it's not fair," said Ripred.

"It is not your city!" said Luxa.

"It may not be yours much longer, either, Your Highness, if such incompetents as Gregor and I do not choose to defend it!" snarled Ripred. "Or have you not kept up on your prophecies?"

"Your defense is no guarantee of anything, or have you not kept up on your prophecies?" retorted Luxa. "And finding you languishing in a pit does little to reassure me of your worth!"

"Stop!" Howard sprang to his feet. "You upset the children. You upset us all. You gain nothing by being at each other's throats."

Gregor looked around. Howard was right. Hazard and Boots stood by Temp, holding each other's hands tightly, worried looks on their faces. The bats were rustling their wings in agitation. Cartesian tossed in his sleep.

"Who are you again?" said Ripred to Howard.

Gregor thought the rat was just trying to be insulting. "Shut up, Ripred. You know who he is," he said.

"No, I actually don't," said Ripred.

"Oh. His name's Howard. He's Luxa's cousin. His dad runs the Fount," explained Gregor.

"Well, all I was going to say was that I thought Howard made a good point," said Ripred. "Fighting gains us nothing, Your Highness. We have much to do if we are to help your friends."

"I do not need your help, Ripred," said Luxa.

"I suppose you can take on the Bane's army your-self," said Ripred.

"The Regalian army will be here in a few days. They will free the nibblers," said Luxa.

"In a few days, there will be no nibblers left to free," said Ripred.

CHAPTER

20

The rat's comment was enough to make Luxa drop her hostile manner. "What do you mean?" she said.

"What do you think the Bane's doing out here, anyway?" asked Ripred.

"We heard him speak. He said he was driving the nibblers to a place from which there is no return," said Howard.

"And did he mention where that would be?" asked Ripred.

"Somewhere outside of the Underland," said Gregor uncertainly.

"In the Uncharted Lands," said Luxa.

"The nibblers could return from the Uncharted Lands. They would only have to retrace their steps," said Ripred. "My dears, there is only one place from which there is no return."

The rat waited while it sunk in.

"Death," Luxa whispered.

"So it would seem," said Ripred.

"Are you saying he means to kill them? All of them?" said Howard.

"That is the general idea, yes," said Ripred.

"But there are thousands of nibblers. They may allow themselves to be driven somewhere, but they will not lose their lives without a fight," said Howard. "How can he kill so many?"

"Now there you have me," said Ripred. "Nibblers are good fighters, when backed against a wall. They outnumber the gnawers here, I would guess, ten to one. It would be bloody, they would lose many lives, but they could overpower the Bane's forces now if they wished to. So, they must believe, as you did, that they are only being moved to a new home. That they are saving their lives by not resisting. But have no doubt about it. The Bane means to kill every last nibbler."

"So say I!" a raspy voice choked out. "So say I!"

They all turned to see Cartesian. He had rolled onto

his stomach and was struggling to lift himself up on his front legs.

Howard hurried to his patient. "Easy now. I will give you something to help you heal." He removed the large green bottle and pulled the stopper.

"We must fight! This is not like the other times. The gnawers do not want this land by the Fount. The humans will not allow them to have it!" said Cartesian.

"Stop, Howard! Let him talk!" exclaimed Luxa. She ran over and kneeled by the mouse.

"He believes he is still at the Fount," said Nike.

"Yes," said Luxa. "Cartesian. Cartesian, I am Queen Luxa of Regalia."

"Oh, the good queen. The good queen," said Cartesian, calming a little. "Tell them, 'Fight now! Fight here by the Fount!'"

"I will tell them," said Luxa, running her hand down his back.

"I told them so, but few will take my side. Most believe the gnawers when they say they will only take us to other lands," said Cartesian. "Do not believe it!"

"No, I do not believe it. I believe you!" said Luxa.

"Why would the gnawers want this land by the

Fount? You humans will not let them keep it," said Cartesian.

"Why would they want the jungle, either?" said Ripred. "No rat would live there by choice."

"So say I!" said Cartesian, and then his fevered eyes locked on Ripred and he went wild at the sight of the rat. "Where are the others? Where are the others?" He bared his teeth at Ripred and tried to attack. Cartesian's broken leg crumpled beneath him. "Where are the others?" he demanded.

"Now might be a good time for that medicine," said Ripred.

"Where are the others?" shrieked the mouse.

Howard quickly dosed Cartesian before he could really lose control. Within a few minutes, the mouse went limp.

Cartesian's words had given Gregor insight into the rats' invasion of the nibbler colony. The mice had argued then, about whether to fight the rats or go quietly. And Cartesian's side had lost. Gregor bet it was Cartesian who had scratched the scythe into the cave wall.

"So, you can believe me and your nibbler friend there, or you can continue to console yourselves with the idea that the nibblers are going to some lovely new life somewhere," said Ripred.

Gregor thought of the baby mice, the twisted bodies beneath the cliff, the Bane's speech. "No, I can't. We've got to find the mice and warn them. Can you travel?" he asked Ripred.

"Yes. I'm a bit stiff, but give me a few miles and I'll loosen up," said the rat.

"I have not agreed to let you join us," said Luxa.

"Fly on ahead, then," said Ripred. "You may miss me when you reach your destination."

A line appeared between Luxa's eyes as she pondered what to do.

"It is better to bend a little than to break, Cousin," said Howard. "We do need him. Let him pay off his debt to you."

"Yes, let me make things even between us," said Ripred.

"I will not be taking orders from you," Luxa snapped at the rat. "You will be following mine."

Ripred shrugged. "Fine. I have given enough orders for a lifetime. You make the plans. Of course, if you'd like my advice at a given moment, don't hesitate to ask."

"Let us go forward, then," said Luxa. "Keep to the gnawer's pace."

They climbed back on the bats and took off, flying at Ripred's running speed. The rat made pretty good time given that he'd been confined to a pit for several weeks.

Gregor was preoccupied with the nibblers. How could the rats kill them all? Drive them off a cliff maybe, like they had in Hades Hall? Drown them? He was pretty sure the mice could swim. Starve them? That seemed like a popular choice in the Underland. Or maybe they would try to infect them with a plague. . . .

After about half an hour Gregor looked down and realized that Ripred really needed a break. He was panting hard and foaming slightly at the mouth. Gregor knew the rat would be too obstinate to ask to stop.

"Ripred can't keep going like that," said Gregor to Luxa.

"It is good for him," said Luxa.

"He's going to have a heart attack or something," said Gregor.

"Do not worry about Ripred," said Luxa.

"You just planning on running him into the ground?" said Gregor.

Luxa leaned over Aurora's wing and watched Ripred struggling to keep up. Then she sat up. "He is too rotten to die," she said.

"Luxa!" Suddenly Gregor had had it with her. "Okay, stop! Everybody land!" he shouted.

"You do not give orders here!" said Luxa.

"Neither do you. Not to me, anyway," said Gregor. He swung off Aurora's back while she was still in flight and crossed to Ares as the bat touched down. Thalia and Temp were piled on top of Ares. "Thalia, can you fly?"

"Yes, if we do not go too fast," said the little bat.

"Ares, can you carry Ripred?" said Gregor. Ares was the one bat who might have the strength to do it.

"I can try," said Ares.

"No, Ares, you do not need to carry that rat," said Luxa.

"Yes, he does," said Gregor. "Thalia, take Temp."

"Oh, now you are in charge?" said Luxa.

"Why does one of us have to be in charge? We were doing fine until you declared war back there and started bossing everybody around!" said Gregor.

"I recall it starting much earlier," said Ripred, dragging himself onto Ares's back. "Even as a baby she was very pushy."

"I am trying to help the nibblers!" said Luxa.

"Really? Well, you're not helping them by hurting Ripred," said Gregor. She scowled and opened her mouth to speak, but Gregor didn't give her time. "And I don't care if that makes you mad, Luxa. Get mad! Don't talk to me! How will that be different from about ninety-five percent of the time, anyway? You're always mad at me for something. Usually, I can't even remember what! What's it matter? I don't live here. I'm just visiting. Anything that I've been doing to help you, that's just a favor! Not something I owe you. And when we get back to Regalia, I'll be sent home and we can forget we ever knew each other! Okay?"

The last word hung in the tunnel. The outburst surprised even Gregor. It was too extreme. Where had it come from? Was it connected to his rager thing? Why had he said it? What, in fact, had he said? He couldn't quite remember, but whatever it was, he could tell by the look in Luxa's eyes that he had actually hurt her feelings.

"Gre-go is too loud," said Boots. She scooted up to Luxa and held her hand protectively. "Shh, Gre-go."

Everyone was staring at him, waiting for his next

move. "I really think this will be faster," said Gregor in a gruff voice.

"Fine," said Luxa, and crossed back to Aurora with Boots trotting beside her.

Howard touched Gregor's shoulder. "Perhaps I will ride with —"

"Yeah, I'll go on Nike," said Gregor. "Don't worry; I'll hold on to Cartesian."

As he climbed up on Nike's back, he felt Ripred's eyes on him. "What?"

"Nothing," said the rat innocently, but Gregor noticed his nose give a deep and distinct sniff.

They did move more quickly now. Gregor tried to justify yelling at Luxa with that thought, but it didn't really work.

A light wind blew over his face. It was more than the usual breeze he caught by just being on a moving bat. The air was warm, too, and smelled more pungently of sulfur. A bit of something blew into his eye and he blinked repeatedly to get it out. It was hard to get any tears going in the wind.

What had he said that had hurt Luxa? It wasn't just that they had argued; they were always arguing. He tried to recall his speech. Something about the nibblers. Ripred. Go ahead and get mad. So, what? "We can forget we ever knew each other! . . ."

That last part. He tried to imagine Luxa saying those words to him and realized how awful it would be. To suggest it would be possible to forget the last year. To forget what they owed each other. Without Luxa, he would have been killed his first night in the Underland. He would never have gotten his dad back. Boots would have died in the rats' maze. And he had done things for Luxa, too. Good things. Things he was proud of. Saved her from the spinners. Helped find the plague cure. He was here now tracking down the nibblers, wasn't he? For better or worse, their lives had wrapped in and around each other since the moment they'd met. He didn't ever want to forget he had known her.

"Nike, can you speed up?" said Gregor. "I need to tell Luxa something."

Gregor worked on his apology as they caught up. "I'm sorry," he thought; that would be a good opener.

Nike's nose was even with Aurora's feet. Hazard was asleep, his head on Luxa's lap. Howard sat with his back to her, holding Boots. Luxa looked at Gregor, waiting.

Gregor swallowed and leaned forward so he could speak quietly. "Look, I just wanted to say, I'm —"

And that's when the currents hit them.

CHAPTER
21

The first blast of air caught Nike from below and tossed her upward, slamming Gregor and Cartesian into the ceiling and pinning them between the bat and the stone. Luckily, Gregor had been leaning forward. His backpack cushioned the blow somewhat, although he could feel the edges of his extra flashlights and the binoculars cutting into his back. His face was pressed into the fur on the back of Nike's head. He struggled to turn his head sideways, so he could at least breathe.

Nike was battling to free herself from the powerful current when it suddenly abated. They dropped down a few feet and the second blast hit them from behind. Nike's wings shut as they shot like a bullet through a gun barrel through several hundred yards of tunnel and then out into wide-open space.

Then the winds took over.

There was not one or two but dozens of currents competing in the cavern. You could see the individual airstreams. Each had the same misty look as the one that had first brought Gregor to the Underland from his laundry room and gave off a faint white light. Gregor was ripped off Nike almost immediately and then buffeted by the currents that accosted him from all sides. He felt like a kite being flown in a storm. A kite whose string had snapped that had no hope of being reeled in.

Fortunately, his flashlight was securely hooked to his belt loop. As he whipped around he caught glimpses of the others. They seemed as helpless as he was.

He panicked for a moment when his flashlight beam revealed the cavern floor fifty feet below. But then he realized he wasn't falling. None of them were. The currents held them aloft, swirling them around like leaves on a fall day.

Gregor got his hand on his flashlight and felt a tiny bit more in control. A particularly strong wave of air caught him from behind and he struggled to break its hold.

Ripred sailed by him with his legs stretched out flat like a flying squirrel. The rat shouted something at Gregor, but he couldn't hear over the roar of the winds. A few minutes later, after slamming into Howard and almost catching Boots as she whizzed by looking puzzled but not particularly upset, Gregor passed Ripred again, flying in the same position. This time Gregor could just make out the rat's words: "Stop fighting!"

Stop fighting? Gregor realized every muscle in his body was so tense, it could snap, because he was, in fact, trying to fight off the wind. To somehow gain control of the currents with his arms and legs. "Stop fighting," he thought. "Just relax!" It couldn't hurt to try. He made an enormous effort to unlock his muscles. It wasn't easy. Every new wave of air made him tense. "Relax!" he ordered himself. "You can't fight it. Think of Ripred!" Gregor stretched his arms over his head and straightened his body out. Suddenly he was not being attacked by the wind; he was being carried by it. He got thrown off course almost immediately but fought the impulse to struggle. "Relax!" he ordered himself, stretching out again. The stream of air swept him along easily. And this time, he understood. If he didn't fight the current, he could ride it. Exhilaration flooded through him. "I'm flying!"

For a minute, he was completely absorbed by his newfound talent. This was nothing like riding the bats, where he was merely a passenger. This was just Gregor zooming around in the sky — well, not the sky — but zooming around in the air like a super-hero. The freedom, the sense of power, was amazing. If he could always have wings, Gregor didn't think he would ever be afraid of any creature the Underland could dish out. He gave out a wild whoop and rode smack into Ripred. Gregor slid down the rat's body but managed to grab hold of his tail and hang on.

"Having a good time, are we?" called Ripred over the wind. "Checked up on your friends lately?"

Instantly ashamed that he was enjoying himself, Gregor shot his flashlight beam around. He spotted Luxa above him, and it was clear she had mastered the trick of riding the winds. She had one-upped him, actually, because she seemed able to move from current to current without losing control. When Luxa rolled sideways to catch another wave, Gregor saw Boots was on her back. The little girl had her arms and legs wrapped tightly around Luxa's body. Temp coasted by with Hazard clinging to his shell. Cartesian was having no difficulty, as the mouse was asleep and riding easily around. Howard was still getting tossed around quite a bit, as he was trying to make his way to the bats. But the bats! They were the ones having the most trouble of all.

Those long, beautiful bat wings were not an asset in this situation. They picked up several competing currents at once. Having ridden milder currents all their lives, the bats could not suppress the instinct to try to navigate these. But every time their wings opened even a foot or two, they'd get spun around like a top. Ares, who was the largest and had the greatest wingspan, was in the worst trouble.

"Ares!" Gregor cried out. He let go of Ripred's tail only to find the rat had reached out and snagged his backpack with his back claws.

"What's your plan?" called the rat.

Gregor had no plan. He was merely following an impulse to help his bat. "I don't know! I don't know!"

"We have to land!" shouted Ripred. "Form a base!"

"Okay!" said Gregor, although he really had no idea what Ripred was talking about.

The rat began to maneuver from one current to another, moving them farther away from the center of the windstorm with each shift. Gregor, who was still being dragged around by his backpack, twisted his head around to see where they were going and realized they were headed straight for one of the stone walls of the cavern. "No!" he cried out, thrashing around to get free before they crashed. But at the last minute Ripred caught another current and Gregor found himself being dragged along the floor of a cave.

"A little trust, please," said the rat in disgust.

"Sorry," said Gregor. He sat up, rubbing his elbow that had been scraped on the floor. Outside the cave, he could see his friends flying around. "Now what?"

"We have to find some way to bring them in. You don't have anything handy like a rope in there, do you?" said Ripred, nudging Gregor's backpack.

"No," said Gregor.

"No," sighed Ripred. "Well, then, I suppose it will have to be my tail."

Ripred positioned himself backward at the edge of the cave, gripping the floor with his claws and letting his long rat tail blow out into the currents.

"Now what do we do?" asked Gregor.

"Wait," said Ripred. "Don't worry, they'll catch on."

Gregor moved his flashlight in a figure eight at the cave mouth to attract attention. Ripred was right. In a few minutes Luxa had made her way through the currents and grabbed hold of his tail. The rat pulled her into the cave and Gregor scooped Boots up off her back.

"Hey, what's going on?" he asked Boots.

"Luxa is a bat," said Boots. "I ride. I fly, too."

"You did a good job," said Gregor. "Now we have to get the others in."

"I can help!" said Boots, and ran for the cave mouth.

As she launched into the air, Gregor barely caught her by the ankle and pulled her back in. "Whoa! No, Boots. I've got a special job for you."

"For me?" said Boots, immediately interested.

He didn't. Gregor considered having her sing again, but that probably wouldn't hold her attention if nobody was falling asleep. He dug in his backpack looking for an idea and came upon the binoculars. "Here," he said. "You're our scout. You look through these and tell us when you see somebody fly by."

It was a pointless task. Between the light the currents put off and his flashlight beam, they weren't having trouble spotting the others. But it gave Boots something to do. "Temp is big. Temp is small. Temp is big. Temp is small," she said importantly as she raised and lowered the binoculars.

"Heads up, here comes the crawler," said Ripred.

Temp sailed in and clamped on to Ripred's tail. The rat hauled him in and Hazard slid off his shell.

"Hazard, are you well?" asked Luxa, hugging him.

"Yes, I am fine. But the fliers are not," said Hazard.

Things looked bad for the bats. They were still being hopelessly tossed around, unable to manage the currents.

Howard made his way in next, dragging in Cartesian by the tail. "I do not know how to get the fliers in," Howard said. "I tried to ride Nike, to help her, but I only added to her difficulties. They are tiring quickly."

"We must do something!" said Luxa.

"We could form a human chain maybe," said Gregor.

"All holding on to my poor tail, I suppose?" asked Ripred. "I'll never be able to manage the lot of you with that wind force."

"We cannot just leave them there!" said Luxa. "I am going back in!"

She was about to dive back into the winds when Ripred blocked her with his tail. "What's your plan?"

"I . . . I do not have a plan," said Luxa.

"Oh, that's too bad," said Ripred. He dropped his tail, but she didn't jump.

"Do you have one?" demanded Luxa.

"I might, if someone asks nicely," said the rat.

"Will you tell me your plan?" asked Luxa stiffly.

"Pleeeease," instructed Ripred.

"Please," said Luxa through gritted teeth.

"All right. Get to the fliers. Start with the little one. Pin her wings down with your legs; you'll have to fight her. I doubt they can help trying to fly any more than you can help breathing. Ride her in," said Ripred. "Don't let her open her wings. Understand?"

"Yes," said Luxa, and dove into the currents.

"Yes, *thank you*!" Ripred called after her.

It didn't take Luxa long to get to Thalia. It took not only Luxa's legs but also her arms to hold down the bat's wings. Then Luxa was able to guide Thalia to the cave. When Thalia came in reach of Ripred's tail, she caught it the only way she could, with her teeth.

"Ouch!" said Ripred, dragging them in. "All right, all right, let go, you little viper."

Thalia unclenched her teeth and lay exhausted on the cave floor.

"I think I can bring Aurora in. I do not know about the others," said Luxa, panting with exertion.

"Do you want me to take Ares, Gregor?" asked Howard. He was a lot bigger and stronger than Gregor. It would make sense for him to have the biggest bat.

"No, he's my bond. I'll do it," said Gregor. He had no idea what he was in for. He made his way out to his bat without too much trouble, switching from one current to the next until he was only a few feet away. Only at that distance did he realize how much Ares was suffering. The bat's body was contorting violently as he tried to break free of the currents. It was as if he was trapped in some horrible force field that would allow him to move only a few feet in any direction before it yanked him back to its center. The thing that unnerved Gregor the most was the sound Ares was making. Not words or the clear, high bat squeaks Gregor could sometimes hear. It was like a scream. A continuous, tormented sound of pain. Being caught in the currents seemed to be literally driving Ares insane.

Gregor felt a hundred times guiltier for having enjoyed flying and not realizing Ares's predicament.

Getting his arms around Ares's neck was the first challenge. Every time Gregor would move into range, one of the bat's powerful wings would jerk out and send him spinning off to the side. It hurt and it prolonged the rescue, because then Gregor had to work his way back to Ares and start all over again. Ripred was right. The bat had no control whatsoever over the impulse to fly.

On about the tenth try, he finally managed to dodge the spastic wings and fasten himself on to Ares's neck. The rest of Gregor's body whipped around wildly. There was no opportunity to lock his legs around the wings. He knew Ares wasn't intentionally trying to shake him off, but that's what it felt like.

"Stop fighting!" he told the bat, just as Ripred had told him. But he wasn't even sure Ares heard him. The screaming continued unbroken and there was no perceptible difference in Ares's body movements.

"Stop fighting! Give up!" ordered Gregor. Still no change. Gregor didn't know how much longer he was going to be able to hang on. Then a fortunate current blew Gregor flat against Ares's back just as his wings shut. Gregor clamped his legs around Ares's sides. "It's

Gregor!" he shouted right into Ares's ear. The screaming cut off, and Ares seemed to be aware of Gregor's presence for the first time. "I've got you! Don't open your wings! Do not open your wings, Ares!"

Now Gregor could feel a different kind of struggle as Ares fought the instinct to open his wings as the different currents struck him. "Overlander . . . I cannot — !"

"Yes, you can. Hold them closed. I'll fly for a change. Okay?" said Gregor.

"O — kay!" said Ares back. "Do not . . . leave me!"

"I won't leave you! I promise!" said Gregor.

It was slow going. Gregor was still pretty shaky at flying on his own. Directing his bat's body through the maze of currents was an entirely new skill to master. Especially since he felt he had to keep talking the whole time, reassuring Ares, reminding him to keep those wings shut. If he took even a slight pause, he could hear the beginnings of the scream starting to build in Ares's throat again.

Gregor had thought they were almost at the cave once, only to turn and discover its light receding from him as another powerful current swept them away. His legs began to shake with the strain of holding down Ares's wings. Gregor needed help, but there was no way to go back for it. No way he could possibly let go of Ares after his promise.

He realized he no longer had the strength to try to guide Ares anywhere. All Gregor could do was hold on. Maybe they'd both just pass out soon and then the others could —

Someone landed behind him. Gregor almost went limp with relief. Then he remembered he was not the one being rescued and reinforced his grip on Ares's wings. Gregor leaned his head against the bat, shut his eyes, and just kept talking, kept talking until somehow they were lying on the floor of the cave.

Gregor released his stiff limbs and turned his head. Both Howard and Luxa were behind him on Ares.

"It took both of us to bring in Nike," said Howard. "We thought you might need a hand."

"I did. Thanks," said Gregor. He looked at Luxa. Remembered that he had been about to tell her something when the currents had knocked him into the tunnel ceiling.

Ripred's nose pushed him off Ares. "Off. Off. Let him breathe."

Gregor rolled off on to his side and wobbled to

his feet. All four bats were lying on the floor, too traumatized to get up.

"Well, there goes our ride," said Ripred in frustration. "It will take hours for them to recover."

"It would help if they could hang," said Howard, running his hands over Nike.

"There's a ledge in the back," said Hazard.

"Good, Hazard. Excellent," said Howard. "Let us see if we can get Thalia on it."

Gregor was not sure exactly what they were doing, but he helped Howard carry Thalia back to a rock ledge and flip her upside down. Her claws immediately fastened on the rim, and her body seemed to relax. On trips the bats usually slept huddled together on their feet, but of course, this was their most natural resting position.

One by one, Gregor and Howard moved the bats to the back of the cave and hung them from the ledge. They shifted their claws only enough to move into a tight line. None of them spoke, but they seemed calmer.

"Rest," Howard said to them. "All is well. Rest."

Everyone gathered near the bats, as far away from the howling winds as possible. Temp discovered some mushrooms that were edible. They broke the mushrooms off the cave wall and ate them straightaway, ravenous from the workout. Then they passed around a water bag.

"To sleep, go you all, to sleep," said Temp. "Watch, will I, watch."

Since there seemed little danger of anything getting into the cave, everyone took him up on his offer.

Sometime later, Gregor awoke to the sound of the others breathing. The wind noise was gone. He could see the outline of Temp, sitting patiently at the front of the cave. As Gregor rolled over, his ear pressed against the stone and he heard another sound. A faint scratching intermingled with a sort of tapping. He sat up and found Ripred awake beside him in the dark.

"I can hear something. Scratching around," said Gregor.

"I know. It's nothing to worry about. Go back to sleep," said Ripred.

Feeling secure under the rat's guard, Gregor did as he said.

Hours must have passed when Gregor felt Howard shaking his shoulder. "Gregor, the currents come and go. We need to move on while they are still."

Gregor was so stiff and bruised, he had trouble getting to his feet. He could only imagine how bad the bats must feel. They were on the ground now, nibbling some mushrooms. Gregor crossed to Ares. "Hey. Are you all right?"

"Yes," said Ares, but his voice was weak.

"We must never be in those currents again," said Nike.

"It is madness," said Aurora.

And Thalia began to cry just at the memory of it. She huddled in Nike's wings miserably.

"Hey, Thalia, I've got a special one for you," said Gregor gently. "What did one wall say to the other wall?"

"I do not know," sobbed the bat.

"'Meet you at the corner,'" said Gregor.

It took a few moments for the joke to sink in, and then Thalia's sobs were interwoven with giggles and finally she was just laughing. A little more shrilly than usual, but laughing all the same. The other bats laughed, too, happy to see Thalia distracted.

They had to move on. Somewhere the nibblers were in peril. Precious time was running out. The bats were still in need of recovery, but it couldn't be helped.

"Do we have any idea where the rats have the mice?" asked Gregor.

"I believe if we follow this cavern we will intersect the path the rats were driving them along," said Ripred.

"Do not fly out into open space. Stick close to the walls. Always keep a cave or two in sight that we may take cover there if the currents resume," said Luxa.

"Now that is a good plan, Your Highness. And how refreshing that you have one," said Ripred. But Luxa was too tired to do more than shoot him a look.

They took off, flying close to the walls. Gregor kept expecting the cavern to end or dwindle into a series of tunnels. Instead it went on and on. It was by far the largest open space he had seen in the Underland, except for the Waterway. He saw his first volcano after about an hour. It was quiet, except for the plumes of smoke that wafted out of its top. They passed others. Some rumbled threateningly. One had a few steady streams of lava leaking from it. None of them were really exploding, but they made the air hot and fetid.

Occasionally the currents picked up and they would quickly dive into nearby caves until the winds died down enough for safe flying. On the good side, after a windstorm the air was usually somewhat more breathable. About the fifth time they headed in for a landing, Gregor thought the bats were overreacting. The currents were barely more than a breeze. Then he realized the stop had nothing to do with the wind.

Ripred ordered them all to flatten out on the floor before he remembered he wasn't in charge. "Sorry," he said to Luxa. "Old habit."

"Do as he says," said Luxa. She was already on the floor, peering out from behind a small pile of rocks. Gregor got on his stomach and then scooted up beside her.

At first, he didn't know what he was looking at. There was a volcano. A golden glow issued from the top. That wasn't a reason for pulling over, though.

Then he heard Cartesian's voice behind him as it whispered, "The others."

CHAPTER

22

Gregor squinted into the ashy gray light and finally made out the nibblers. They were walking single file down a long curved path that began at what looked like the mouth of a tunnel high in the rocks and that led to a pit at the base of the volcano. On one side the path ran along the edge of a sheer cliff with sharp rocks at the base. A stone wall ran along the other side of the path, blocking the view of the pit from their sight. It wasn't until the nibblers were almost at the bottom that they realized where the rats were sending them.

The nibblers who had reached the pit began to squeal out warnings to those following them. Gregor could see the alarm spreading up the path. Mice turned and tried to force their way back up, some literally crawling over the backs of the others to try to reach the tunnel at the top. A handful made it only to be driven back by rats. Then the mice began to shriek as a large boulder was rolled into place, sealing the mouth of the tunnel. They threw themselves against the boulder but could not budge it.

"Let us go!" cried Luxa, jumping to her feet.

"And do what?" asked Ripred, stepping in front of her. "You, all of you, you've got to stop running into dangerous situations without using your heads! There is no faster way to get killed!"

"We can carry them out of the pit to safety!" said Luxa.

"Yes, a handful of them. But there are hundreds trapped down there. Do you not think the rats might notice an airlift going on? And then what? We lose the one element we have in our favor. Surprise," said Ripred.

"Then what do you want us to do?" demanded Luxa. "Wait for the volcano to smother them in lava?"

"I want you to think about it a moment!" snapped Ripred.

"*V* is for volcano," Boots reminded everyone. "And valentine." She poked Ripred on the haunch with her scepter. "Valentine!"

Ripred sighed. "Why are you here?"

A gust of wind swept by, drawing everyone's attention. "Oh, great. The currents are starting up again," thought Gregor. If they became too strong, the bats wouldn't be able to navigate them. At least they were clearing the air a little. One overriding current seemed to be blowing out of a nearby cave. It was sweeping the ashy haze toward the nibblers and giving Gregor his first breath of clean air in hours.

"Look, the nibblers are taking action," said Howard.

The mice had overcome their initial panic and were organizing themselves to carry out an escape plan. They had begun to build a pyramid by bracing themselves along the far wall of the pit. A single row of mice formed the base. Others were swarming onto their backs swiftly. The pyramid was rising before their eyes.

"That's smart. A pyramid," said Gregor.

"No, it is the Isosceles Maneuver," said Cartesian.

Gregor looked at him. For the first time since Cartesian had joined them, the mouse seemed lucid. "What's that?" Gregor said.

"It is not a true pyramid, for it has three, not four, points. Rather, they aspire to mimic a two-dimensional triangle," said Cartesian.

"Oh," said Gregor. It seemed to him that at home almost anything with people standing on top of other people was called a pyramid, but he didn't feel like arguing the point with Cartesian, especially after all the mouse had been through.

"See, they have a plan. Let's work with it," said Ripred. "What they need is someone to hold that path if the rats come through."

"Then we will do so," said Luxa.

"Agreed. Temp, watch the pups. The rest of you mount up," said Ripred.

Gregor was about to jump onto Ares when Ripred stopped him. "No, I'll need him to get to the path. Ride with someone else and change over when he drops me off."

"Here, Gregor," said Howard. He extended a hand and pulled Gregor up behind him on Nike.

"We should wait until the boulder begins to move. That will give us time to reach the path but not alert the rats to our presence beforehand," said Luxa.

"Good. Very good. Now you are thinking," said Ripred. "Everyone wait for it, as she says."

They sat watching, tense and poised for takeoff.

The mouse pyramid was nearing the top of the pit.

Soon they would be able to begin freeing themselves. Still the boulder didn't budge.

"If there were to be lava, would we have some warning?" asked Howard.

"Generally, I believe there's a rumbling, some sort of sound," said Ripred. "Although I am no expert."

The first nibblers began to climb over the edge of the pit. The escape plan was working.

"Maybe the rats won't come back," said Gregor. "Maybe they didn't figure the mice could get out."

The mice were sending the pups up now. Trying to save them first. When five little ones had reached the top, a pair of full-grown mice began to corral them away from the pit as fast as possible. No rats appeared to interfere.

Back in the tunnel, they watched silently for a few more minutes.

Then Luxa broke the silence. "Something is wrong. Why would the rats allow this?"

"They wouldn't," said Ripred. He paused. "Unless they were expecting something else to do their work for them."

"But there's no lava. The volcano isn't even erupting," said Gregor.

Suddenly Temp began to wave his antennas, his feet stepping nervously on the ground. "Not lava, it be, not lava," said the cockroach.

"What is it, Temp? What's wrong?" asked Gregor. One thing he had learned from past experience: If Temp was alarmed, there was good reason.

"Not lava, it be . . . it be —" Temp did not know the words for it. He broke off and began clicking in agitation.

"What's he saying, Hazard?" asked Gregor.

"I don't know. It doesn't make sense. I think he's saying the volcano is breathing," said Hazard.

Boots puffed out her cheeks and blew a stream of air in Gregor's face. "Like this. It goes breathing like this." She blew again. "Like balloon goes out."

"The nibblers. Something is happening to them!" said Howard.

Gregor squinted to make out the scene in the distance. His eyes flew to the boulder first to see if the rats had pushed it aside, but it was still fixed in place. He scanned the mice. They looked okay. They looked fine. Then one mouse at the top of the pyramid fell. Then another. Then the entire pyramid disintegrated.

Every last mouse left in the pit had collapsed in a

heap. But they weren't dead. He could see their bodies flailing around.

Chaos broke out in the cave.

"What is going on?" cried Gregor.

"We must go!" cried Luxa.

"Not go, you do, not go!" begged Temp.

"Take flight, Aurora!" insisted Luxa.

Aurora seemed as eager to go as her bond. She extended her wings to take off. With lightning-fast speed Ripred leaped at the pair, flipped Aurora onto her back, and threw himself across her body. Luxa, who was trapped under Aurora's shoulder, yelled at him furiously, but Ripred completely ignored her.

Gregor upended his backpack, dumping the contents on the ground, and snatched the binoculars. He trained them on the mice and felt his heart start to pound.

"What do you see, boy? What's happening to them?" said Ripred.

Gregor stammered as he tried to describe the nightmare unfolding before his eyes. "I don't know! They can't! They —" The mice were rolling on the ground, pawing at the air, at their necks, their bodies wracked with terrible spasms. "They can't breathe!" he finally burst out. "They're suffocating!"

Luxa was screaming like a maniac. Hazard pushed on Ripred's shoulder, trying to move him. "Let her up! Let her up!"

Howard grabbed Hazard and forced the boy's face into his shoulder. "No, Hazard. She cannot go. She cannot help them," he said. Tears streamed down his cheeks.

Now they could hear the desperate screams coming from the pit. Cartesian limped to the cave opening and tried to fling himself into the air, to either catch a current to help the other nibblers or simply kill himself. Gregor didn't know which. But Ares caught Cartesian before he fell.

"It's poisonous gas," said Ripred. "It must be leaking from the volcano."

"But I can't see it! I can't see anything!" said Gregor. His hands shook as he tried to adjust the binoculars.

"It has no color," said Howard.

"Nor odor that I can detect," said Ripred, his nose twitching furiously. "Of course, the wind carries it away from us — will you hold still!" he growled at Luxa. "Temp, are we in any jeopardy here?"

"Heavy, the poison be, heavy," said Temp.

"Then it's all settling in the pit," said Ripred grimly.

When Gregor saw a pup, gasping to draw air, fall lifeless from its mother's back, he had to drop the binoculars. But now that the currents had cleared the air, the nibblers' agony was visible from the tunnel. They went into convulsions, teeth snapping on empty air, claws lashing out to battle an enemy they couldn't see.

"Nike, can you shield Thalia's view?" said Howard. "She has seen too much!" Nike enveloped Thalia in her wings.

"Come here, Boots!" said Gregor, scooping up his sister and laying his hand over her eyes to block the gruesome scene, although it did not seem to be upsetting her. She wriggled to get free.

"No, Gre-go, I want down!" said Boots.

"Get off of me!" Luxa freed her sword and stabbed it into Ripred's shoulder.

"Aah!" cried the rat, leaping back. Blood poured from the wound. His gums pulled back, showing his newly sharpened teeth.

Aurora righted herself and Luxa sprang to her feet, Ripred's blood dripping off her blade.

Gregor dropped Boots and was pulling his sword to step between them when Ripred snarled at Luxa,

"Fine, you stupid brat! Fly right into it and get your-self killed!"

"Shh," said Boots, putting her forefinger to her lips. "You are too loud."

Luxa spun around to the cave mouth, preparing to mount Aurora. Then Luxa saw the mice and froze, one hand clutching the fur at her bat's neck.

The screams had faded away. Here and there was a bit of movement. Then all was still.

The only sound in the cave was Howard, softly weeping.

"Shh," said Boots, patting him. "Shh. The mouses are sleeping."

CHAPTER

23

"They sleeping? Right, Gre-go?" asked Boots, frowning slightly.

"That's right, Boots," said Gregor, trying to keep his voice steady. "They're sleeping." This was what he always told her when something died. Even if they found a dead bird on the playground, he'd tell her it was asleep and then pick it up with an old newspaper or something and hide it in the trash when she wasn't looking. Later she'd see it was missing and be happy it had flown away to its home. And Gregor would act happy with her. If he couldn't tell her that a pigeon had died, there was no way he could tell her about the mice.

"I know. They take a nap. Like in the song," she said, reassured.

"That's right. Like in the song," said Gregor.

"Ripred. Is there anything we can do?" said Luxa hoarsely. "Please."

"No, Luxa," said Ripred. Gregor thought this was the first time he had ever heard Ripred call her by name. "Nothing can be done for them."

"May I see your glasses, Gregor?" she asked.

Gregor was reluctant to give her the binoculars. It was bad enough from a distance. Magnified, the scene was even more horrific. "They're not really working," he mumbled. But she took the binoculars from his hand and pointed them at the mice.

"So this is it," she said. "This is how they plan to kill them all."

"Without the nibblers resisting," said Ares.

"You may let me go," said Cartesian quietly, and Ares released him. The mouse curled into a ball and buried his face.

"I thought they would starve the nibblers, attempt to drown them perhaps. But this . . . this has no precedent," said Nike.

"This has too much precedent," said Ripred grimly. He began lapping away the blood from his shoulder.

"Let me," said Howard. He gave Hazard to Luxa

and got out his medical kit. "It is not too deep," he said, examining Ripred's shoulder.

"It's deep enough," said Ripred, shooting a look at Luxa. "I consider my debt paid. My life for your life."

"Yes. Paid in full," said Luxa.

Everyone sat there stunned, watching Howard bandage Ripred's wound. They avoided looking out where the murdered mice lay in the pit.

Gregor could not make sense of what had just happened. He had seen death before, plenty of it. But nothing like this. It was not just the number of dead. When they had fought the ants in the jungle, the ground had been covered in corpses. But that had been a battle, with two armed forces facing each other. It had been horrible, but at least everyone had had a fighting chance to survive. What had happened to the mice . . . trapped in the pit . . . unable to even defend themselves against the gas . . . not just soldiers but everyone, even the pups . . . it was murder on a grand scale. It was a massacre. And probably only one of many.

Only Boots seemed unaffected by what had just occurred. "Hazard dances with me?" she said, tugging on her friend's hand.

"No, Boots, I cannot," said Hazard.

"I dance myself," said Boots. She began singing as she spun in a circle.

> "DANCING IN THE FIRELIGHT
> SEE THE QUEEN WHO CONQUERS NIGHT.
> GOLD FLOWS FROM HER, HOT AND BRIGHT.
> FATHER, MOTHER, SISTER, BROTHER,
> OFF THEY GO. I DO NOT KNOW
> IF WE WILL SEE ANOTHER."

Gregor vaguely wondered if he should stop her. It seemed disrespectful to the nibblers. But he could not seem to speak.

Boots turned into a mouse now, pawing the air and spinning here and there.

> "CATCH THE NIBBLERS IN A TRAP.
> WATCH THE NIBBLERS SPIN AND SNAP."

It was too awful, watching her dancing around like a mouse after what they had just witnessed. With Cartesian lying beside him. "Stop it, Boots," Gregor said, but she was caught up in the song. She curled right up on the ground and pretended to sleep.

"Stop it!" repeated Gregor, more harshly than he had intended. He grabbed her by the arm and pulled her to her feet. Her lips pressed together and he could see tears filling her eyes. Gregor hugged her close to him. "Sorry, I'm sorry. It's just not a good time for dancing," he told her.

"Mouses do dance," she said. "I just do dance like mouses."

"I know," said Gregor. "You didn't do anything wrong."

"I want to dance like the mouses do dance," said Boots, sniffling.

"It's okay. Don't cry," said Gregor, stroking her curls. He guessed the writhing of the mice had looked like a dance from the distance. In fact, the words from the song:

CATCH THE NIBBLERS IN A TRAP.

WATCH THE NIBBLERS SPIN AND SNAP.

They very accurately described what he had just seen. . . .

QUIET WHILE THEY TAKE A NAP.

Gregor turned and took in the lifeless bodies in the distance. If you didn't know they were dead, like Boots you'd think they were taking a nap. The words of the song began to drum in his brain.

> *CATCH THE NIBBLERS IN A TRAP.*
> *WATCH THE NIBBLERS SPIN AND SNAP.*
> *QUIET WHILE THEY TAKE A NAP.*

"She's right," he said aloud.

"How so?" asked Ares.

"That song. That part about the nibblers," said Gregor. "We just watched it happen."

> *FATHER, MOTHER, SISTER, BROTHER.*

Whole families had died out there.

> *OFF THEY GO. I DO NOT KNOW*
> *IF WE WILL SEE ANOTHER.*

They wouldn't see another, if the Bane had his way. He was determined to kill them all and —

"That's not a song," said Gregor suddenly. "That's a prophecy! Don't you see?"

He could tell by the expressions on their faces that they didn't. It had been a song so long, for hundreds of years. It was like someone telling him that "Hey Diddle Diddle" would explain a train wreck in Nevada. But Gregor had not grown up singing the song and doing the happy little dance that accompanied it. To him, the words were still new, and now they were sinister.

"Sandwich wrote it, right?" said Gregor. "He carved it in the nursery."

"Yes, he carved it in the nursery, not the room of prophecies. And we do not know who wrote it, it is so old," said Luxa.

"It didn't come from the Overland. We don't have nibblers. It's from down here and Sandwich made it up and it's happening now!" said Gregor, totally convinced. "We just watched the nibblers get caught in a trap and dance all around and take a nap, only it isn't a nap, not the kind you wake up from! 'Father, mother, sister, brother, off they go'! To die! Don't you see?"

The others didn't look convinced, but Ripred pushed aside Howard's hands and began to pace. "What is it? That nonsense in the first verse. How does it go? Someone sing it!"

Hazard's high voice piped up.

"DANCING IN THE FIRELIGHT
SEE THE QUEEN WHO CONQUERS NIGHT.
GOLD FLOWS FROM HER, HOT AND BRIGHT."

"That's enough. 'Dancing in the firelight . . .'" The rat stared out at the glowing volcano. "We've got firelight, anyway."

"'See the queen who conquers night,'" said Nike. "Luxa, you could be the queen."

"I am not dancing," said Luxa. "Nor have I been."

"Maybe it's not the queen who dances," said Howard. "Things may be said to dance in the light. When it flickers. Someone's eyes, water, anything really. . . ."

"The nibblers danced in the firelight," said Aurora.

"We still need a queen," said Ripred.

"'Gold flows from her, hot and bright,'" said Ares. "Luxa has no gold."

"I have nothing but rags," said Luxa, looking down at her tattered clothes. "I cannot be the queen."

There was a low but unmistakable rumble. Everyone's head turned to the volcano. A thin stream of lava bubbled out of the top and ran down the side toward the pit. As gold as gold can be.

"'Gold flows from her, hot and bright . . .'" said Nike. "You do not think —"

"I think the Overlander's right," said Ripred. He nodded at the volcano. "There's your gold."

"And there's your queen," said Gregor.

CHAPTER
24

A second, louder rumble shook the ground under their feet. "Get out of here!" shouted Ripred.

Everything fell into confusion as they tried to mount the bats. They had changed riders so many times during the trip that no one was sure where their designated seat was. Gregor grabbed Boots and jumped on Ares, only to remember that no other bat could carry Ripred. He slid off and slipped on a battery, which was lucky, because it reminded him to scoop all the stuff he had dumped out earlier into his backpack and sling it over his shoulder. By that time, Boots had run off and had climbed on Temp's back.

"Stop!" called out Ares. "Luxa, Hazard, Gregor, and Boots on Aurora. Howard, Temp, and Cartesian on Nike. Thalia, fly under me in case you tire." He assumed the takeoff position and said to Ripred, "Let us go."

Everyone stumbled around but by following Ares's directions managed to get a seat. Gregor ended up at the front of the bat with Boots hugging him around his neck. Hazard and Luxa swung up behind them.

The second the bats left the cave they were swept up in the strong current that was blowing in from a cave overhead. It was the same current that had cleared away the ashen air and assured that the poisonous gas did not drift their way. Now it was carrying them directly toward the glowing volcano.

Gregor was afraid the bats were going to flip out again, but they were doing all right. It was not one current that overwhelmed them but the convergence of multiple airstreams that had occurred earlier. Almost immediately he felt Aurora turn away from the volcano and begin to head into the wind. It was so strong, they made little forward motion. He wrapped his arms around Boots, trying to block as much of it as possible. Switching tactics, all the bats suddenly whipped back around and flew straight for the volcano. At first it seemed insane, but then Gregor realized that the only way they could get away from the volcano was by riding the current that blew right over it.

Between the force of the wind and the bats' own wing power, they were moving through space at an incredible velocity. The volcano, which had been a distant vision, quickly rose up in front of them.

Gregor was awestruck by the "queen." She was majestic and imposing but most of all furious. Clouds of steam hissed from fissures in her sides. Molten lava oozed out of her top and flowed downward in fiery streams. Even with the wind whistling in his ears, Gregor could hear her rumbling growing into a roar.

As they flew out over the volcano, Gregor could see the bubbling lake of lava brewing inside. The air seared his lungs. Everything was suffused with a hot red light, including the pit where the dead mice lay. Gregor pressed his cheek against Boots's so she couldn't turn her head in the direction of the mice. But he forced himself to look at the bodies, to keep the image clear and alive in his brain. He knew he had to be able to tell their story, and tell it as fully as he could, when he returned to Regalia. He had to be able to impress upon people the magnitude of what had happened. Was happening. So much counted on it.

Gregor began to feel dizzy. Some of the fumes rising out of the volcano must be riding along the current with them. He knew the fumes must be affecting the bats as well, but none of them showed any sign of slowing. They left the volcano behind as quickly as they had approached it.

Another ominous rumble rattled the earth below them. Gregor was feeling sicker, not better, as they flew on. What if they were just riding along in a pocket of poisonous gas and it was only a matter of time before they were overcome? He tightened his hold on Boots.

"You okay, Boots?" he hollered over the wind.

"I sleepy," she said. "I take a nap."

"Oh, no. No naps!" shouted Gregor, alarm shooting through him. "You stay awake, okay?"

"Okay," said Boots faintly, but he could feel her trying to nestle up against him.

"A tunnel! Find a tunnel!" he heard Ripred shout.

They were approaching a giant stone wall that signaled the far end of the cavern. The bats began to dodge in and out of openings on the wall, trying to judge what was merely a cave and what might be a tunnel and a means of escape.

Above him Gregor saw Nike begin to circle at an opening. Howard was waving his arms wildly for them to follow. Aurora made straight for the tunnel. Nike disappeared inside it first, followed by Ares, who now had Thalia locked in his claws. Aurora brought up the rear.

Gregor immediately felt safer when they entered the tunnel. The air was still nasty, but at least they were out of the volcano's reach. He relaxed his grip on Boots a little and was just turning to check on Luxa and Hazard when the "queen" erupted.

Nothing else could account for the deafening explosion, which rattled his teeth, sent flares of color shooting before his eyes, and left him unable to hear anything but a shrill ringing in his ears.

A blast of hot air hit them and then there was no air, only a stinging cloud of ash and dust that blocked out everything else. He struggled to breathe, to see, thought he must pull Boots's T-shirt up over her face to protect her. He could feel himself losing consciousness and felt Luxa's grip on his shoulder loosening. "No," he wanted to cry out. "Hold on! Hold on! Boots!" That was the last thing he remembered. . . .

When he came to, Gregor was lying facedown on

what felt like a large rock. His chin hung off a sharp ledge. He began coughing immediately. As he sat up he could feel the ash falling from his body, sending up a cloud, making it even harder to breathe. He staggered forward a few steps and fell off the rock hard, landing in at least four feet of ash. Struggling back to his feet, he began to wade through the stuff, waving his hands blindly in front of him. His head pounded so badly, he thought the pain might actually split it in two. Making it to a wall, he braced himself and vomited until nothing but bile came from his stomach. Trembling and disoriented, he leaned against the wall and tried to clear his thoughts.

"What happened?" he thought. He remembered the volcano . . . flying . . . a vision of the mice glowing in the red light . . . light . . . he needed light. . . .

Gregor fumbled for the flashlight at his belt and found the switch. At first he thought it was broken. Then he realized the plastic face was obscured by ash. He knocked the flashlight against the wall and wiped it as best as he could on the inside of his shirt.

The light revealed a large tunnel blanketed in gray dust. It had drifted into deep banks like snow in places. In others, just a fine layer covered the floor. Gregor waded to a relatively clear spot to try to get his bearings. He must have passed out and slipped off Aurora's back at some point. But then where was Boots? She had been in his arms. Where were Luxa and Hazard? Where were the others?

"Where are the others?" Gregor remembered Cartesian's panicked cry. "Where are the others?"

Gregor plowed back to the rock, dragging his feet through the ash, trying to locate anyone else who might have fallen with him. By the time he had covered the area, he was choking on a cloud of dust but had discovered no one. He started down the tunnel in the direction his head had been pointing when he awoke, hoping that he might find the rest of the party ahead.

The smooth surface of the ash was unbroken by footprints. It muffled his footsteps, making them barely audible to his still ringing ears. He had never felt so alone in his life. Never had been, probably. There was no sign of life anywhere. It was a miracle he was even alive, that he had not suffocated in the eruption. Probably he would have if his chin hadn't been hanging off the rock. If he'd landed on the ground, most likely he'd have been buried alive and died under the ash.

"Where are the others? Where are the others?" Cartesian's voice screamed in Gregor's brain.

What if none of them had survived? What if they had all fallen unconscious to the tunnel floor? Maybe he was passing by them as he shuffled along, unaware of their bodies under . . .

Gregor stopped and pressed his palms against his eyes. "Don't. Don't think like that. Just keep walking. You just keep walking."

It was impossible to gauge how much time was passing. The tunnel remained unchanged. His breath came in short ragged gasps. Every inch of him, inside and out, seemed coated in a layer of ash.

He remembered the water in his backpack and popped it open. The first mouthful he just swished around his mouth, rinsing the grit from his teeth, and spat on the floor. Then he took a long, deep drink, not bothering to ration it. Feeling slightly better, he trudged on.

At some point, he became aware of a faint breeze on his face. "Another current," he thought, and wondered if he should try to take cover behind a rock. But the breeze remained gentle and carried air that was definitely sweeter than what he'd been breathing.

It eased the pain in his chest and the ache in his temples.

He thought the twinkle of light in the distance was only a reflection of his own light. But when he directed his beam to the ground, he could still see it there. He moved faster, causing more dust to rise. "Hey!" he tried to call. "Hey!" But he couldn't even hear his own voice.

Then he could make out a figure, as ghostly and gray as his surroundings. He caught glimpses of the light again, brighter now. Gregor broke into a run, more like a clumsy gallop really, because his knee had been damaged when he stepped off the rock.

"Hey!" he called again, and this time he heard himself and the figure turned.

Gregor stopped short. One look at Howard's face confirmed what Gregor had been dreading. Someone was dead.

"Who is it?" said Gregor, his heart slamming against his chest. "Not Boots?"

Howard stepped aside, squinting at the gray figures before him. Boots was all right. She was sitting on Temp's back, holding her scepter with its tiny light.

At first glance, everyone looked all right. Ripred, Cartesian, Luxa, Hazard, the cluster of four bats. But he had miscounted. Only three bats huddled together.

Lying on the floor, almost obscured by the dust, her head cradled in Hazard's lap, was Thalia.

CHAPTER
25

"Oh . . . not Thalia," he said. Silly, laughing little bat. But brave, too. Going under the river water to retrieve Hazard. Trying so hard to keep up with the full-grown bats. Still trying after the flood and the scorpions and the nightmarish currents.

Gregor thought of the last joke he'd told her. "What did one wall say to the other wall?" And how her frightened sobs had turned to giggles at the punch line. "Meet you at the corner." She was barely more than a baby really.

He walked over and knelt by Thalia's side. She looked so tiny, with her wings folded against her. Without that bright bubbly thing that was Thalia radiating from inside her. He gently laid a hand on her chest, brushing away some of the ash, revealing a small patch of peach-colored fur.

Hazard wept inconsolably, his tears raining down on Thalia's face. "It was the mark. The mark of secret. It took my mother and now it took her."

Under the gray powder, Luxa's face was still and distant. "It was my fault," she said. "I should never have allowed any of them to come on the picnic."

"The picnic was not the danger, Cousin," said Howard. "I was the one who insisted on trying the Swag, and it was there our troubles began."

"No, I did not fly fast enough," said Ares. "I had her, but I did not fly fast enough."

"Stop it, all of you," said Ripred. "She died from poisonous fumes, not by any of your hands. She was flying, so she breathed deeper. She is small, so she succumbed more quickly. None of you are to blame."

The whole episode was beginning to worry Boots. She slid off Temp's back and came over to Thalia. "Wake up! Wake up, Thalia!"

"Don't, Boots," said Gregor, catching her hand.

"She needs to wake up," said Boots. "Hazard is crying. When does she wake up?"

Gregor could not find it within him to give his standard reply. To pretend that in a short time Thalia would be back with them, laughing and happy. And somehow it seemed wrong to try. Boots was getting older. Very soon, she would begin to realize the truth on her own, anyway. "She's not going wake up," he told her. "She's dead."

"She doesn't wake up?" said Boots.

"No, not this time," said Gregor. "This time, she had to go away."

Boots looked around at all their faces, at Hazard crying. "Where did she go?" No one had an answer. "Where is Thalia when she doesn't wake up?"

The question hung in the air for an eternity. Finally, it was Howard who spoke up. "Why, she's in your heart, Boots."

"My heart?" said Boots, putting both hands on her chest.

"Yes. That's where she lives now," said Howard.

"She can fly away?" asked Boots, pressing her palms tightly against her heart as if to keep Thalia from escaping.

"Oh, no, she will stay there forever," said Howard.

Boots looked up at Gregor for confirmation. He gave her a nod. She went back over and climbed onto Temp's shell thoughtfully.

"If you mean to do something with her, do it now. We cannot stay here long or this dust will finish us all," said Ripred.

"I will take her," said Ares.

"Hazard, you must say good-bye now," said Luxa.

"No!" cried Hazard. "No! You can't take her! I won't let you!"

And then an awful scene followed where they literally had to drag Hazard from Thalia so that Ares could take her body away. To where, Gregor did not know. There was no comforting the little boy. Howard finally got a dose of sedative down his throat between wails, and his sobs quieted.

Ripred sent Aurora and Nike ahead to scout for a less toxic area. While they were gone, Howard cradled Hazard in his arms and rocked him back and forth. "You know, I lost my bond, too," said Howard. Thalia and Hazard had not been officially bonds, but it seemed a minor detail now. "Pandora was her name."

"What happened to her?" asked Hazard.

"We were on the Waterway. She flew out over an

island and was attacked by mites. They killed her," said Howard.

"Couldn't you help her?" asked Hazard.

"No. I wanted to. Even when she was lost I still wanted to try. But there was nothing I could do," said Howard. "Nothing but cry, just like you are crying now."

"What was she like?" asked Hazard.

"Funny. And curious. She always had to be the first one to see something new. And she loved to eat shellfish," said Howard with a smile. "Great big piles of them."

Gregor thought of the slimy shellfish Howard had kept insisting were a delicacy, and wondered if his passion for them had anything to do with how much he associated them with Pandora.

"You're not crying about her now," said Hazard.

"No," said Howard. "I have become used to carrying her in my heart."

"My heart is so crowded already," whispered Hazard. "But I'm sure the others will make room for Thalia. She is not a very big bat." And with that, he drifted off to sleep.

Gregor thought about all the others Hazard had

lost . . . his mother, his father, Frill . . . and now Thalia had gone to join them. . . .

They were all silent for a while. No one wanted to be responsible for waking Hazard up and bringing him back to this aching reality.

Finally Ripred spoke to Gregor. "Well, at least you showed up. Thought we'd lost you for good."

"I'm all right," said Gregor. "What happened?"

"Not exactly sure. You blacked out and fell. Fortunately you had the sense to push your sister onto the bat's head," said Ripred. "Ares tried to go back for you, but we had no idea where you were and the ash was so deep."

"I'm all right," Gregor repeated, although this was one of the worst days of his life.

Aurora and Nike flew up. They had discovered a tunnel that led upward to cleaner air. Everyone could squeeze on to the two bats, except Ripred, who said he would wait for Ares, anyway, and then follow their trail. It was only a short flight to the passage. The higher they traveled the sweeter and cleaner the air got. Eventually they broke free of the tunnel and came out on a rock formation with a flat top and vertical sides. Fresh breezes washed over them. A cold spring burbled out of a crack and fell hundreds of feet, where it disappeared into a dimly lit tangle of thick vines.

"We're back at the jungle," said Gregor.

"Yes, it borders the Firelands," said Howard.

They took turns gulping down the spring water and washing the ash from their skin. Boots said she was hungry, and Howard gave her the last piece of stale bread. She curled up next to Hazard on a blanket and went to sleep. Cartesian had fallen into some kind of stupor as well, although he often sat up and looked around, squeaking rapidly, before collapsing back on the ground.

No one else seemed able to sleep. Or talk. They just sat around, staring at the flashlight, or down at the jungle. Gregor watched Luxa watching the spring for a while. She seemed unnaturally calm.

About an hour later, Ares arrived with Ripred. "Where did you take her?" Howard asked.

"Back to the queen. So she might lie with the nibblers and not alone," said Ares. "The lava will claim them all soon. Half were already covered."

"Yes. The Bane does not only want to kill them. He wants them to disappear without a trace," said Ripred.

"So, it seems the Overlander was on to something about the song."

"You mean that it's a prophecy," said Gregor.

"If it is, we should name it," said Aurora.

"I have already done so in my head, but the name need not stick," said Nike. "I call it 'The Prophecy of Secrets.'"

"It is well named," said Ares. "Since the marks of secret led us to it."

"And even its nature was a secret," said Howard. "No one suspected our childish song to be a prophecy."

"One we still need to break," said Ripred. "I think we understand the first two parts now. We know who the queen is. We know about the nibblers. How does the last part go?"

Luxa spoke the last verse. Without the playful melody, they were just words. And loaded words at that.

> "Now the guests are at our door
> Greet them as we have before.
> Some will slice and some will pour.
> Father, mother, sister, brother,
> Off they go, I do not know
> If we will see another."

"I suppose the first question is who the guests are?" said Howard.

"Well, if the door opens to Regalia, which I'm assuming since Sandwich called it 'our door,' then given the circumstances, the guests are probably someone Her Highness has recently declared war on," said Ripred.

"The gnawers," said Luxa. "And we will greet them as we have before."

Gregor remembered that this was the part in the dance where everybody pretended to pour tea and serve cake.

"*SOME WILL SLICE AND SOME WILL POUR.*"

"What does that mean?" he asked.

"Swords slice," said Luxa. "And when the city is under siege, we pour boiling oil over the walls and onto our enemies."

She said the words without any particular sense of fear or revulsion. But Gregor was filled with both.

"I wonder when the attack will be," said Howard.

"Someone must return at once to warn the Regalians," said Nike.

"No point in me coming, of course. Neither side

would welcome me. No, I think I may hang around here for a while," said Ripred.

"And do what?" asked Gregor. Ripred always had a plan.

"Those nibblers we saw today . . . they're only a fraction of the ones who've been driven here. The others might still be alive. I was thinking . . . they'd make a likely army," said Ripred.

"For you?" said Luxa. "They would never follow you."

"That's where you come in, Your Highness," said Ripred. "If we go together, we might be able to mobilize them."

"I might alone. What do you add to the mix?" asked Luxa.

"Don't be impertinent. Is it yes or no?" said Ripred impatiently.

Luxa only took a second to consider the proposition. "Yes," she said. "Howard, will you come?"

"I will have to, Cousin, if you insist on doing this," said Howard doubtfully. "Cartesian will want to join us."

"He's too beat up," said Ripred. "But with you two

on fliers and me on the ground, we might be able to break them out."

"I am sure they will follow me, if we can get in close enough for them to hear my voice," said Luxa.

"I'm counting on that," said Ripred. "Let's say four hours' rest, and we begin."

Gregor had begun feeling like he was invisible. No one was involving him in the plans at all. "I'll be ready," he said.

"No!" Ripred and Luxa spoke in the same breath and with the same intensity.

"What?" said Gregor in surprise.

"Not you, boy. You're taking the pups back to Regalia," said Ripred.

CHAPTER

26

"No, I'm not!" said Gregor. "I'm going with you!"

"You cannot!" said Luxa. Her eyes darted around as if she was trying to find a reason. "What about Boots and Hazard?"

"I don't know, they can ... Howard, you could take them back," said Gregor.

Ripred, Howard, and Luxa exchanged glances. Gregor had an awful realization. They didn't want him to come. They were thinking about how he had choked in the fight with Twirltongue and they thought he would fall to pieces again.

"You don't think I can fight," he said bluntly. "Well, fine, okay. Maybe I did freak out when I lost my light, but it's not really dark here, with the volcanoes and all and I think there's been a few other times when I've shown that —"

"It's not that, Gregor. Everyone knows you can fight. Far better than I can," said Howard.

"Then what? You're still mad at me?" he asked Luxa.

"No, I am not," said Luxa.

"So?" said Gregor.

"Has he not been told anything?" asked Howard.

"About what?" said Gregor in frustration.

"Just this. You've got to get back to Regalia. Now that the war's begun, you're of no use to us without your sword," said Ripred.

Gregor's hand went to his hip in confusion. His fingers wrapped around the hilt of his weapon. "I've got a sword."

"Not any sword. Your sword," said Ripred. His eyes narrowed. "You didn't lose it in the tunnel, did you? When you fought Twirltongue?"

"What?" said Gregor, totally confused. "Yeah, I lost that sword. I threw it behind me at the rats. So, what? There's, like, thousands of them."

"No, Gregor. He means the sword Vikus gave you. Sandwich's sword," said Howard.

"Oh, that," said Gregor. It was true, Vikus had tried to give him an impressive, jewel-studded sword that had once belonged to Sandwich, but Gregor had refused to take it. He knew where it was, though. It was in the museum, which had always seemed an odd place to keep it, since the museum held items from the Overland. It was on a shelf wrapped in the same silken cloth that Vikus had originally presented it in. For the first time Gregor wondered if Sandwich's sword was there because everyone believed it belonged to him now, whether he had accepted it or not. "That's not really mine."

"Yes, it is. It says so in that prophecy I mentioned to you, about killing the Bane. 'The Prophecy of Time,'" said Ripred.

"And it says I need Sandwich's sword?" asked Gregor.

"Among other things. I had assumed Vikus had at least let you know of the sword's importance. That you were destined to inherit it," said Ripred. "That we all believe it is your sword. Any of that sound familiar?"

"No. He just seemed happy I wouldn't take it," said Gregor.

"Ever the optimist, your grandpa," said Ripred to Luxa and Howard.

"Yes. Perhaps we should arrange for him to spend a bit more time in the field," said Luxa grimly.

"Listen to you," Ripred said with a chuckle.

"Do you know what he said when we were taken prisoner by the spinners that time? He said he thought things would be different because of some recent trade agreements he'd made with them," said Luxa. "I was eleven and I knew that was idiocy."

Ripred grinned. "He might have been right."

"We might have been dead," said Luxa.

"We *would* have been dead if it wasn't for your grandpa," said Gregor, suddenly protective of Vikus. "The spiders were going to kill me until I mentioned his name."

"Yes, yes, you don't have to defend Vikus. But the sword. You know where it is?" said Ripred.

"Yeah," said Gregor.

"Good. Go back and put it in your belt and don't let it leave your side again," said Ripred.

"What is the big deal about telling me about the prophecy?" said Gregor. "I've been through four of them now. How much worse can they get?"

"We didn't really know if it was going to happen. Some thought certain events were supposed to occur. But after today, it seems they have," said Howard.

"And?" said Gregor.

"And no one wants to tell you because . . . the odds are . . . look, we don't even know if we're interpreting it right," said Ripred. "We're usually wrong, aren't we?"

Gregor knew he could no longer wait for Vikus to explain things. "What's it say, Ripred?"

"It says . . . well, it suggests . . . you're probably going to —" Ripred broke off abruptly. "Vikus will tell you. That crazy girl, what's her name? Nerissa. Ask her about it. She'll explain it better than me," said Ripred.

"But I —" said Gregor.

"No!" said Ripred. "You ask in Regalia. As soon as your bond is rested, you can leave. Take the pups and Cartesian and Temp."

"To fight, I stay, to fight," objected Temp.

"No, Temp," said Luxa, kneeling before him. "I would wish you at my side, but we have much greater need of you at home. You must go to the crawlers, tell them what has happened, and rally them to our cause."

Temp shifted back and forth on his feet in indecision.

"And I beg another favor as well," Luxa continued. "I need you to look after Hazard now as you have looked after Boots for Gregor. I put him in your care."

"My care, the boy be in, my care?" said Temp in surprise.

"If you will take him. For there is no one among us who perceives danger so quickly and accurately as you do," said Luxa. "Or meets it with such courage."

This was true, as they had all found out the hard way. Temp had warned them against exploring the island with the mites, they had ignored him, and Howard's bond, Pandora, had been eaten alive. Temp had warned them not to wander into the jungle after the sweet odor of fruit, they had ignored him, and one of the rats, Mange, had been swallowed up by a carnivorous pod. Temp had warned them about the volcanic gas, Luxa had ignored him, and both she and Aurora would have ended up poisoned if Ripred hadn't listened. Yes, this was true, but . . .

Gregor flashed back to the girl he had met when he

first arrived in the Underland. The girl who had made fun of the roaches . . . their slowness, their inability to fight, their cowardliness . . .

She had certainly come a long way.

"You, so say, you?" said Temp.

"I, so say, I," said Luxa. "Will you do this, Temp?"

"Yes," said the cockroach.

"Thank you," said Luxa. She laid her hand on his head and his antennas gave a quiver. It was the only good moment in a very dark day.

Gregor volunteered to watch while the others slept. He was just going to spend the next day riding on Ares, anyway. Luxa said she could not sleep and walked off to the edge of the rock. She sat, her legs hanging in space, unimpressed by the sheer drop below her. The sadness on her face made Gregor's heart ache. He couldn't seem to take his eyes off of her. It didn't matter. She didn't even notice. But someone else did.

"What's the story with you and the queen?" said Ripred softly.

"Nothing," said Gregor. "I thought you were asleep."

"You've become very fond of her," said Ripred.

"I don't know. I guess," said Gregor.

"You want a piece of advice?" said Ripred.

"Don't bother. I know what you'll say. The whole thing's stupid," said Gregor.

"Quite the contrary. I was going to say that life is short. There are only a few good things in it, really. Don't pretend that one isn't happening," said Ripred.

It was the most un-Ripred-like advice Gregor could imagine. Was the rat just making fun of him? No, he sounded on the level.

"That's crazy. I mean, it's not like the two of us could ever . . ." Gregor didn't even know how to finish the sentence.

"Boy, there's a war on. We might all be dead in a day or two. I wouldn't project too far into the future if I were you," said Ripred. He gave a gigantic yawn. "Well, I'm done in." He circled around three times and lay down. In less than a minute he was snoring.

Gregor sat there a few minutes more, watching Luxa. Then he found himself walking over to her. He hadn't figured out what to say to her, how to tell her that he cared about her, about what happened to her. So he just sat near her. Off to one side, but not hanging his legs off the edge. After all the hours in the air, he still avoided heights.

Luxa spoke first. "Those nibblers in the pit. They were not from the Fount. They were from the jungle. Many of them were my friends. I saw several of the pups born. I even named one."

She hadn't cried yet. Neither had he. Not about the nibblers or about Thalia. That would come later. If there was time.

"They love mathematics, you know," she said. Gregor didn't particularly know that, or much else about the mice, but he didn't say so. "So, I called him Cube."

"That's a good name," said Gregor.

"He was in the pit today," said Luxa. "I recognized his marks."

A light breeze blew over them, warm and muggy and bringing up the smells of the jungle below them. Gregor's thoughts shifted from the victims in the pit to Hamnet and Frill, who had died in the jungle during the battle with the ants. He wondered if the vines had grown over their bodies. Probably by now . . .

"Gregor, I was thinking about what you said in the tunnel," said Luxa. "About you being only a visitor here."

"Forget about that. I was just going off," said Gregor.

"No, listen. You were right," said Luxa. "When you get back to Regalia, no matter what people tell you, you have no obligation to stay. This is not your world or your war," said Luxa. "If you were to return home after you read the prophecy, I would not hold it against you."

"This must be some prophecy," said Gregor.

But she avoided the topic and went on. "To even involve you in the nibblers' plight was unfair of me. You owe them nothing."

"I didn't try to help them because they owed me anything," said Gregor. "What was happening to them was wrong."

"But when you see what the prophecy demands of you, that may not be enough," said Luxa. "I declared the war for the nibblers' sake. You share no history with the nibblers. We humans here have many reasons to be indebted to them. What have the nibblers ever done for you?"

The breeze ruffled her hair, pushing it back from her face, giving him a clear shot of her eyes. They were asking for an answer. Needing to know if she could count on him.

"They saved your life," he said.

And for just a moment, Luxa's face softened and she smiled.

CHAPTER

27

Gregor insisted Luxa try and rest. He didn't want her going into battle dropping with fatigue. She resisted at first, and he had to threaten to wake Ripred for backup. "And then, he won't shut up until you're begging to sleep," said Gregor.

"All right, then, all right," she said. She laid down with Hazard and Boots and he was gratified to see she soon drifted off.

Gregor went back to being on guard. He didn't have a watch or any means of telling the time. But it wasn't a problem. Ripred woke himself up at what was probably precisely four hours and roused everyone but Hazard, Boots, and Cartesian.

The mouse began to stir as they readied themselves and soon was on his feet. When he found out about the plan, he was determined to join the party to liberate the nibblers.

"I must go! I must find Heronian! You will need her to break the code!" insisted Cartesian.

"Heronian? I'll keep an ear out for her. But you're going to Regalia," said Ripred.

An argument ensued and was about to get ugly when Howard suddenly shouted, "Enough! Cartesian is right. They are his family, his friends. He must be allowed to go! But first . . ." Howard dug through his medical kit and removed a small reddish bottle Gregor had not noticed before. He held it up to Cartesian. "But first you must take a dose of this. It is an elixir of potent herbs to give you strength."

Cartesian gulped down the liquid without hesitation, blinked a few times in confusion, and then fell to the ground like a stone.

"What did you give him?" asked Gregor.

"A very powerful sleep agent. We use it only rarely, when a patient must lose consciousness immediately so that we can operate. To remove a limb or some other drastic measure," said Howard. "Was this wrong of me?"

"Quite the contrary. But obviously, the rest of us

need to keep an eye on you," said Ripred, only half-joking.

They loaded Cartesian, Boots, Hazard, and Temp onto Ares's back. Gregor rinsed out his water bottle and filled it with clear spring water. He placed it in his backpack with the binoculars, duct tape, batteries, and all the flashlights, even the one he usually wore on his belt. Then he slid the backpack around Luxa's shoulders.

"What is this?" she asked him as he adjusted the straps. While the supplies from Regalia were common property on trips, Gregor's backpack was always treated as if it was exclusively his.

"I don't need it. You might," he said. "You know how to change the batteries in the flashlights, right?"

"I think so. But what will you do for light on the way back to Regalia?" she asked.

Gregor held up Boots's scepter and hit the on button. "I've got it covered."

When they hugged good-bye, there was one moment where he thought he wouldn't let go. But he did. He embraced Howard, too. Kind of patted the bats. Nodded to Ripred since the rat wasn't particularly physical unless he was knocking you down.

Then Gregor climbed up on Ares. He took them all in . . . Luxa, Howard, Nike, Aurora, and Ripred . . . knowing there was a good chance, a really good chance, he might never see them again.

"Run like the river, boy," said Ripred.

"Fly you high," said Gregor back. But it was Luxa's face he could not take his eyes off of as Ares lifted into the air.

He lay down between Boots and Hazard and put an arm around each of them. Temp sat at his feet, to watch over Cartesian.

Gregor turned off the scepter to save whatever light might be left in it. The thing had already performed way beyond expectations. For a while, there was a faint aura from the jungle below. Then it was pitch-black.

He wanted badly to sleep, knew he needed to. But sleep did not come. The darkness made him highly sensitive to sound. Sometimes he would hear a rushing stream or a cry from some kind of animal, but mostly there were the sounds they carried with them. The flap of Ares's wings, Boots's soft breathing, and Hazard's ramblings in his drugged sleep. Gregor caught words here and there . . . Thalia . . . mother . . . secret . . .

Secret. The very word filled Gregor with weariness.

How exhausting it was to keep a secret, to hide a secret, to discover a secret, to know a secret existed and waited for you in the dark.

This summer had been nothing but secrets. The scars on his legs that no one in New York could see. The clandestine visit to Queenshead. The hidden mark of the scythe under Cevian's body. Lying to Vikus about the picnic. Sandwich's concealing the prophecy as a song. And the worst secret of all . . . the truth of what the rats were doing to the mice.

There was another secret waiting back in Regalia — at least it was a secret to Gregor — about what Sandwich had written in "The Prophecy of Time."

But Gregor didn't think it was as big a mystery as his friends imagined. No one could even begin to tell him the truth about it. So he could only assume one thing. That in no uncertain terms, the new prophecy called for death. Either his own, or that of someone he deeply loved. What else could make even Ripred stumble around for an explanation when it was mentioned?

A new sound filtered through his thoughts. The sound of claws, rat claws, against the stone surface below him. Gregor rolled over onto his stomach and looked over Ares's shoulder, but of course he could see nothing without light. The rats picked up on their presence, though, smelling them, even recognizing Gregor's scent because they were screaming his name, calling for his death.

In a few minutes, it was quiet again.

"How many were there?" Gregor asked Ares.

"Six or seven hundred," said Ares.

"Heading to Regalia or the Firelands?" said Gregor.

"Regalia," said Ares.

"Do you think the Regalians know the rats are coming?" said Gregor.

"I do not know," said Ares and his wings began to beat even faster.

Gregor thought of the unsuspecting city lying in wait, of all the people, of his mom in her hospital bed . . . and Ares could not go fast enough.

By the time the bat had reached High Hall, it was clear no one knew about the approaching army of rats. They were waved through the gate without any special clearance, although they did get some worried looks. No extra guards were posted. In the city, people were going about their regular business.

The instant they landed, Gregor ordered the guards

to take the rest of his party to the hospital. "And tell Vikus the city is about to be attacked by gnawers."

Before they could ask any questions, Gregor took off down the hall. His knee was swollen and pain stabbed him at every step, but he didn't stop. He knew his way around the palace now. It didn't take long to get to the museum.

Sandwich's sword was in its usual place, still carefully wrapped in cloth. It hadn't been touched since he'd last seen it. He reached for it and something caught his eye. Mrs. Cormaci's camera. He'd put it in here after the party, so it wouldn't get broken or anything. Beside it was the stack of photos he'd taken the day of Hazard's party. His mom had suggested Gregor take them home and put them in a special album for Hazard.

He couldn't stop himself from lifting the photos. On the top of the stack was the first picture he'd taken of a beaming Hazard and Thalia. It was only about a week ago, but it seemed like another lifetime. Now Hazard was crazed with grief and Thalia lay dead in the pit with the nibblers. Five of his friends were on a desperate mission in the Firelands to warn the nibblers and try to assemble an army. Rats would surround the city in a few hours, fueled by the Bane's hatred.

Gregor's hands began to tremble. A few of the photos fell to the ground. He quickly scooped them up and found himself looking at one he'd never seen. Who had even taken it? It was a picture of him dancing with Luxa. The camera had caught the moment where he lifted her up in the air. They were both laughing. He remembered just how happy he'd been. . . .

Then the trumpets began to blare out their warning. Frightened voices called to one another in the hall. Everyone knew now. The rats were coming.

Gregor tucked the photo of the dance in his pocket and piled the rest on the shelf. He pulled the sword from his belt and tossed it away. The soft, silky fabric was cool on his hands as he unrolled Sandwich's sword. The sight of it, covered with jewels and intricate carvings, took his breath away. He had forgotten how awesome it was.

He hesitated a moment. To take up Sandwich's sword. But why? He had already made his choice, back when he had watched the mice dying in that cloud of poison gas. He would fight because he could think of no other option. But what would that mean for him, the warrior? Who would he be . . . if he survived . . . who would he be when he laid down Sandwich's sword?

No, not Sandwich's. It was his now. His hand grasped the hilt and he made a few cuts in the air. A deep, satisfying swish accompanied each movement. It was heavier than he expected but perfectly balanced. It made every sword he'd ever held seem like some cheap plastic thing you might wear as part of your Halloween costume. He slid the blade in his belt, letting his hand rest on the hilt, feeling its weight, its rightness. Something new welled up inside him. A sense of power he was not accustomed to. It came from wearing the sword. "Don't let it leave your side again," Ripred had said. Gregor didn't think there was any danger of that.

"Have you found all that you need?" Vikus's voice was infused with sadness. He had never wanted to give Gregor the sword in the first place.

"Yeah," said Gregor without turning to see him at the door. He tightened his hand on the jeweled hilt. "Yeah, I think I've got it."